J-fie

SOMETHING SPECIAL

Special Note to Parents:

Please note that chapters 6 and 7 contain sensitive material on eating disorders in children. It would be helpful to go over these sections with your child. For more information, refer to the following websites:

Overview of Eating Disorders in Children:
http://www.healthyplace.com/eating-disorders/main/overview-of-eating-disorders-in-children/menu-id-58/
Eating Disorders: Know When to Seek Help for Your Child:
http://www.healthyplace.com/eating-disorders/main/eating-disorders-know-when-to-seek-help-for-your-child/menu-id-58/
Helping Parents Deal With Eating Disorders:
http://www.healthyplace.com/eating-disorders/main/helping-parents-deal-with-eating-disorders/menu-id-58/
Overcoming Eating Disorders:
http://www.healthyplace.com/eating-disorders/treatment/overcoming-eating-disorders/menu-id-58/

Stephanie Perry Moore

SOMETHING SPECIAL

Morgan Love Series
Book 3

MOODY PUBLISHERS

CHICAGO

Edited by Kathryn Hall
Interior design: Ragont Design
Cover design and image: TS Design Studio
Author photo: Bonnie Rebholz
Word Searches by Pam Pugh

Some definitions found at the end of chapters are from WordSmyth.net.

Library of Congress Cataloging-in-Publication Data

Moore, Stephanie Perry.
    Something special / Stephanie Perry Moore.
        p. cm. -- (Morgan Love ; bk. 3)
    Summary: Morgan tries not to be cruel as her classmates are, but an unkind remark gets her in trouble at home and school and it is not until she goes to Vacation Bible School that she comes to appreciate people's differences.
    ISBN 978-0-8024-2265-1
    [1. Teasing—Fiction. 2. Vacation Bible schools—-Fiction. 3. Conduct of life—Fiction. 4. Christian life—Fiction. 5. African Americans—Fiction.]
    I. Title.
PZ7.M788125Som 2011
[Fic]—dc22
                                        2010050843

Printed by Bethany Press in Bloomington, MN – 05/11

1 3 5 7 9 10 8 6 4 2

Printed in the United States of America

For
My Paternal Aunt
Carriebell Roundtree Hayes
(Born September 2, 1948)

I remember the summers at
Grandma Violas being a time of joy.
You played a key role in those treasured memories.
Each year you made me red velvet cake,
and you told me I was special.
Because of the love you gave me at a young age,
I've found my way as a woman.
I hope every young reader has relatives who tell
them they are worthy of greatness
just like you did for me, so they'll always
know they are someone special.

Morgan Love Series

1 - *A + Attitude*   978-0-8024-2263-7
2 - *Speak Up*   978-0-8024-2264-4
3 - *Something Special*   978-0-8024-2265-1
4 - *Right Thing*   978-0-8024-2266-8
5 - *No Fear*   978-0-8024-2267-5

Contents

Chapter 1

Cruel World

"Our class has got this! We're gonna win Field Day! Come on!" Trey said, as he tried to cheer us on.

"Yeah," Billy said. "Look at Mr. Wade's class. We gotta go against them in the relay race. And look at that big girl over there. She looks like a hippopotamus!"

Everyone in my class started laughing but me. I didn't even know who they were talking about, but I knew deep inside of me that it was wrong to laugh at people. It's not fun being on the outside looking in, and two times this year I was on the outside. When my classmates laughed at me, it hurt worse than when I skinned my knee really bad in recess one day in my kindergarten class.

At the beginning of the school year, I got a lot of attention because they kept telling me that I was smart. But now it seemed like nobody cared that I was smart. And that doesn't feel so good. It shouldn't matter that no one thinks I'm special, but seeing that there are two other ways to get attention—I needed one of them.

For one, you had to be really cute, like my friend Brooke. A lot of people started paying extra attention to her. At first, she always wore her hair up in a pony tail, but lately it's been flowing down her back. And it's pretty too. A perm makes my hair pretty, but not like Brooke's. She has hair like a baby doll.

The other way people stand out in the class is if they make jokes and act funny so kids will laugh. But I'm not good at poking fun at people. It's not that I want to be such a good girl; I just don't think hurting anybody's feelings is the right thing to do.

Finally, it was my turn to run in the relay race. And, guess what? It was between me and the girl who was bigger than everybody else in the second grade. Her name is Tara.

Billy handed me the baton and shouted, "You'd better smoke her, Morgan!"

We took off running. Right away, Tara started breathing hard, and I just kept going. We had to run really far, and when I reached the finish line, Tara was nowhere in sight. Though I didn't want her to catch up with me, I hoped she was okay.

Both of our classes didn't even wait to see if she was all right. They just started cracking jokes about her until I didn't wanna hear anymore.

"Maybe if she let some air out of that balloon she could

run faster," one boy said.

"Don't sit beside her at lunch. She'll eat her food and yours," another girl said.

They kept laughing at her as she finally made it to the finish line. The kids in Tara's class were really mad at her too. I didn't say anything and just moved along with my class.

"I'm so glad you beat that girl. If you had let that big girl beat you, we would never let you hear the end of it," Billy told me.

It was time to take a water break, and I saw Tara standing alone with tears in her eyes. I went over to her, wanting to say something nice.

"What?" she asked me. "You got some more jokes you wanna say to me? I'm standin' right here. So you don't have to talk behind my back."

"I wasn't makin' jokes about you," I said to her.

"You were laughin', and that's just the same. You think I'm happy about my size? I know I'm the biggest girl in second grade. I don't need kids laughin' about it. It's not even my fault."

"What do you mean?"

"At home it's just my mom, my older sister, and me. My mom works late so she's never there when we get out of school. She brings home fast food, and I'm eating at ten o'clock every night. By that time I'm starvin'. So I eat too fast, and I don't take time to **digest** my food. The doctor said eatin' late isn't a good idea. But when you haven't had

11

much to eat all day, you take what you can get," Tara explained with a sad look in her eyes.

I really wanted her to know that I cared about her feelings, so I asked, "Have you tried exercising?"

"Sometimes I try. But when I do, people around me laugh like they're perfect and I'm not."

Tara was getting more and more upset. "Why are people always tryin' to pick on me? They need to leave me alone. Everyone has somethin' they need to work on. I think it's mostly their **character**." Then she shoved by me and walked to her class.

Just then, Brooke and Chanté came over to me.

"What did that big girl want?" asked Brooke.

"Don't call her that!" I snapped back.

"Well, she is a big girl," Brooke said, spreading her arms and making wide circles.

Very sadly, I said, "You guys made her cry."

"Well, she needs to lose some weight," Chanté said, with no sad feelings for Tara.

"What if she's tryin' to lose weight but it isn't working? What if she doesn't have **healthy** foods at home so she can eat right? How would you feel if you had people makin' fun of you all the time?"

"Why would people laugh at me?" asked Brooke. She added proudly, "I look good!"

I just shook my head and walked away. My two best buddies weren't listening to me at all. We had hurt someone's feelings and they didn't even care.

I wished I could take back all of the insults and jokes that Tara heard that day. But the only thing I had wanted was for me to be popular. We were all being mean by only caring about ourselves. Jesus wouldn't be pleased with how any of us were acting.

● ● ● ● ●

"If Alec is going to be my partner, then I'm not doing it," Trey said boldly. Miss Nelson was pairing us up for the three-legged race.

There were three other second grade classes, and our class was in the lead with the most points. We didn't lead by much, and two classes were trailing us close. If we didn't win the three-legged race and tug-of-war, then we would lose Field Day. We all had to work together if we wanted to win.

Right after Trey spoke up, Billy called out, "Me either. If he's in the three-legged race, then I'm not doing it."

"Same for me," Brooke said, as she stood by Trey. He smiled wider than if he was getting his teeth cleaned at the dentist.

Miss Nelson handed Alec the tie he was supposed to use in the race, but Alec threw it down. "No big deal. Everybody knows I'm the best athlete in this class. Win or lose without me—I don't care!"

Even though he said he didn't care, Alec sure looked like he was hurt. He was really upset. His voice was usually strong, but it didn't sound that way now. Alec started to walk off, but I stood in his way before he could go far.

"Wait! Alec, we need you," I pleaded.

Trey huffed and said, "No, we don't."

"Alec, where are you going?" Miss Nelson called out, as he dashed around me and took off.

Walking away from our class, Alec hollered back, "I'm not playin' with them!"

"Get back here, young man," Miss Nelson said to him. But he just sat down on a nearby concrete stump.

When Miss Nelson went over to talk to Alec, I turned and asked Trey, Brooke, and Billy, "What's wrong with y'all?"

"Don't even start, Morgan. That boy pushed us around for months. The last thing I wanna do is be his friend or be tied up next to him. He might trip me and make me fall just for the fun of it," said Trey.

I said, "But you gotta talk to him."

"I don't gotta do anything."

But I wasn't ready to give up, so I tried again. "I'm sure if you talked to him, you'd see."

"See what?" he asked.

Ugh! I just blew out real hard, rolled my eyes, and folded my arms. There was so much more I knew about Alec than anybody else, but my parents wouldn't like it if I ever said anything. I knew that Alec's dad had lost his job and that made him turn into a really mean person. So, I felt bad for Alec. Their dad had screamed and yelled at Alec and his brother so much that they turned around and were mean to other people.

Because I understood why Alec had acted the way he

did, I wasn't mad at him anymore like the rest of them. And if Trey knew, he'd stop being mad too. Besides, the other kids in my class wouldn't be upset with Alec if Trey changed his mind about all this. I wanted all the meanness to stop. I wanted us to have some peace as a class. But I didn't know how to make that happen. I didn't know how to help us all be friends. This was so hard.

"Why do you keep takin' up for him, Morgan?" Billy asked. "You must like him or somethin'."

"I don't like boys . . . not like that anyway." I shook my head at Billy's crazy idea.

Trey looked over at Brooke, and she smiled. I didn't know what was going on, but Brooke and I needed to talk. Everything Trey said, she went along with. She really had no excuse for being mad at Alec. I forgave her, and she should forgive him. Besides, Alec was mostly mean and stuff to the boys more than the girls.

"Brooke, can I talk to you?" I asked.

"No," Trey answered for her. "She's gonna be my partner in the three-legged race."

I grabbed her hand real tight and said, "Trey, you be Billy's partner."

"Ouch! Morgan, that hurt," Brooke said. I let go of her hand when we were away from the others.

"What's goin' on with you, Brooke?"

"What do you mean? I don't like Alec, and you shouldn't either. He didn't even tell Trey he was sorry."

"How do you know that?"

15

"Well, Trey said he didn't."

"Alec needs friends too, Brooke."

"Alec should've thought of that before he was mean to everybody."

"I forgave you, and you need to forgive somebody else. Think for yourself, and stop doin' what other people want you to do."

"Morgan, I'm glad we're friends again, but you want me to think like you. You want me to be just like you. You're talkin' about me following Trey but you want me to follow you. I don't wanna be Alec's friend right now, and that's my choice. He wasn't a nice person, and I'm not going to be nice to him because you want me to. Okay? Now the race is about to start. Are you going to be my partner so we can go after the other team and win the race?"

I nodded and followed her over to where everyone was getting ready for the race to take place. When I looked over at Alec, he had his head down. I was still **determined** to find a way to make him feel like part of our class. Yes, he'd been mean, but there was a reason. Most of the class was just being rough on him, and they needed to stop. After all, we were going to the third grade soon and we needed to start growing up a little more.

When I thought, *what would Jesus do?* I knew the answer right away. Bottom line: I was not going to give up on Alec. And if Jesus were here in person, He would help us all to act nice toward each other. So since I was here, I had to be like Him.

• • • • •

Since we were having so much trouble getting along with each other, we lost the three-legged race. Now our class was tied with Mr. Wade's class. The tug-of-war contest would crown the champions of Field Day.

There was a ten-minute break before the big event. Our class still wanted to win, so everyone huddled around so Trey could give us a pep talk. It wasn't my idea, but I went along with it.

"Okay, now. We need to get our act together, guys. We need our five strongest boys and our five toughest girls out on the rope. We gotta win for the class. We can do it! All we need to do is **participate** and pull together so we can win!"

Before he could finish telling us what to do, which was getting on my nerves because nobody made him class captain, Miss Nelson stepped into the middle of our group.

"Guys, you have one classmate who's sitting over there alone and wants to join in. The rule is that everybody is supposed to participate in at least one event, and Alec hasn't done one. Somebody had better go over there and talk to him, or the coach will **disqualify** our team."

Miss Nelson didn't even have to ask twice. I dashed right over to Alec. I didn't care what anyone else had to say or what they thought about it. But, as soon I got to him, he let me know that he didn't want to hear what I had to say.

"What do *you* want?" Alec said, turning his back to me.

I stepped over in front of him and said to his face, "Alec, we really need you so we can win."

"No, you don't. You're just sayin' that to make me feel better."

"No, really. Miss Nelson just said that everyone has to participate in at least one event or we can't win. I'm not makin' this up."

"But they don't want me, and I don't wanna be anywhere I'm not wanted."

"I've seen you and your brother playin' all kinds of games in the neighborhood. You know you're the bomb athlete, Alec. Why would you let someone tell you that you're not?"

"Because . . . I deserve it! Okay?" he said, just before he got up to walk away from me.

But I wasn't going to let him get away with it. "No! Let's talk, Alec. Why do you have to run away and act like such a baby?"

He stopped and turned back to me. "Why do you care anyway, Morgan?"

"Because if they just knew everything that happened to you then they'd know why you acted the way you did."

"No way! I'm not tellin' them any of my business. Think about it, Morgan. My dad was goin' through a tough time, and he was hard on me. But he didn't come to school with me and treat people bad. I did that on my own. And if it wasn't for how I treated people, then maybe I'd have some friends. But maybe next year will be better. I'm tired of actin' tough and I wanna change. I wanna be nice so kids will like me."

He was making a lot of sense. Just because someone was rough on you didn't mean you had to be rough on other people. Maybe sitting over here alone had helped him to think about it.

"Have you told them that you're sorry?" I asked.

He shrugged his shoulders like he didn't know.

"What kind of answer is that?"

"I don't know. I tried to talk to them but they don't wanna talk to me. I probably said I'm sorry. Why?"

"You don't have to make anybody like you, Alec. But if you really wanna make friends, then be real. Talk to people. Haven't you been bored sittin' here by yourself watchin' Field Day all day by yourself and not havin' any fun?"

"Yeah. We could've won that three-legged race," Alec said with a grin.

"Okay, so can we do tug-of-war now, please?" I asked, just as I heard Miss Nelson calling both of us.

He smiled and said, "Cool."

We jogged over to the rest of the class. Miss Nelson put Alec and Trey at the back of the line. I was in front of Trey. Brooke was in front of me. Billy was in front of her. The rest of the kids, along with Chanté, were closer to the front.

Waiting for the whistle to blow, we were holding on tight.

"You know I don't want you to play, right?" I heard Trey say to Alec.

"Yeah, but you like to win even more. And with me on the team, we can win."

The next thing we knew, the coach, Mr. Bradley, blew the whistle.

"Pull!" Billy yelled out. "We're goin' forward, pull back hard!"

"I don't care if we lose," Trey said, not really meaning it.

"Hey, man," Alec told him. "I'm sorry I hurt you. There was a lot goin' on at my house, and let's just say I've got a lot to learn. But I won't mess with you anymore, I promise. Besides, you showed me somethin'. I'm not the only tough guy at school."

Trey laughed at that. "Yeah. I was tired of you pushin' me around and tellin' me what to do."

"Well, let's just say I got the message," said Alec.

Finally, when the two of them stopped talking, I said, "Okay, so y'all need to pull! We wanna win!"

Then Trey and Alec both pulled as hard as they could. Everybody was trying really hard. We kept pulling until Mr. Wade's class crossed over the line—and we won! Hooray! Miss Nelson's second grade class was the Field Day champs, and all was right with the world!

After the game was over, Trey started talking to Alec, and everyone else did too. Alec, Trey, Brooke, Billy, Chanté, and I went to the cool-off area to get some snow cones. We had earned them, and we were ready to enjoy those flavored ice drinks. They're so yummy!

As the group stood around the table eating our icy reward, the special education class was finishing their last race. I hadn't spent a lot of time with kids who have special needs. But a few of the kids were standing around the table with us, waiting on their cool treats. Some of the kids in our group started laughing at this one kid named Tim. As he ran toward us, one of his knees bumped up against his other knee. The kids were making one joke after another about him.

"Freak!" Some girl called out that **cruel** word, as Tim made it to the snack table.

Everyone started laughing at that. I really don't know why I did it, but I laughed with them and said, "Yeah, he really is a freak." I guess I was trying too hard to fit in with the other kids.

The next thing I knew, Tim was standing in front of me screaming and knocking over the treats. He knew we were all laughing at him, and he had heard me call him that terrible name. It didn't matter that another girl said it before me. In his mind, it was all my fault. I felt bad that I was part of such a cruel world.

Letter to Dad

Dear Dad,

I hope you are taking good care of yourself. I've learned that I can't eat late at night. I need time for my food to **digest** before I go to sleep.

School is almost over, and today I learned a lot about what **character** is. I know that you must be a good person at all times. But I helped people today and I hurt people too. This one girl is not **healthy** and needs to lose weight. The class picked on her, but I tried to stand up for her. But later I made fun of a boy with **special needs**.

I was **determined** to do better, and I got Alec to join us in the tug-of-war game. That was good because the principal would **disqualify** us if we didn't let Alec play. The class learned we all needed to **participate**, and we won.

Kids can be **cruel**, Dad. I'm one of those kids, but I'm trying to be better.

> Your daughter,
> A lot to learn, Morgan

Word Search

```
R  E  A  D  U  N  G  G  O  O  D  B
O  O  K  S  T  H  A  T  S  B  S  T
R  J  Y  F  I  L  A  U  Q  S  I  D
E  P  A  R  T  I  C  I  P  A  T  E
S  E  H  M  Q  U  H  C  P  E  P  N
O  R  E  O  U  C  A  R  A  Z  A  I
L  R  A  R  I  X  R  E  P  I  T  M
U  Y  L  G  L  D  A  U  A  R  C  R
T  S  T  A  T  E  C  L  E  P  I  E
I  J  H  N  S  M  T  B  J  L  C  T
O  A  Y  D  I  G  E  S  T  Z  I  E
N  M  O  M  O  O  R  E  L  E  A  D
```

CHARACTER

CRUEL

DETERMINED

DIGEST

DISQUALIFY

HEALTHY

PARTICIPATE

Words to Know and Learn

1) di·gest (dī-jĕst) *verb*
To break down food so it can be used by the body

2) char·ac·ter (kăr'ək-tər) *noun*
A person's behavior showing goodness and honesty

3) health·y (hĕl'thē) *adjective*
Being well and not sick

4) de·ter·mined (dĭ-tûr'mĭnd) *adjective*
Showing purpose; intent; having a firm goal

5) par·tic·i·pate (pär-tĭs'ə-pāt') *verb*
To take part in something

6) dis·qual·i·fy (dĭs-kwŏl'ə-fī') *verb*
To keep someone or something from joining a team or group for not following the rules

7) cru·el (krū'əl) *adjective*
Causing pain or suffering

Chapter 2

Trouble Costs

"Morgan Love! What did you say to Tim to make him so upset?" Miss Nelson hurried over and asked me.

It was such a weird feeling. I felt like I was spinning around and stuck in a strange dream. I didn't know what came over me. Some kids were laughing because I was in trouble. Brooke and Chanté were upset and didn't want to see me in trouble. Knowing I was in big trouble, I was in shock.

It only took a few minutes for things to change. Just as quickly as we had won Field Day, everything went wrong. Wanting to be cool, I was trying to be with the in-crowd. So I laughed at Tim and repeated a bad name about him. Why didn't I know that my actions would hurt his feelings? And now the choice I had made was going to hurt me.

"Morgan, I'm talking to you," Miss Nelson said, tapping me on the shoulder. "You need to give me an **explanation** for what happened! The principal is on her way over here, and Dr. Sharpe is going to want to know too."

Before I could answer her, the principal walked up. "What is going on here? Why is Tim upset?" Dr. Sharpe asked.

Snow cones were all over the ground, and Tim was down there smashing cups and flavored ice. He was really making the whole scene worse.

Dr. Sharpe helped Tim to his feet, and everyone tried to calm him down. Pointing toward me, he kept shouting, "She joked at me! She joked at me!"

"Is that true, young lady? I want you to tell me the truth."

Our principal remembered that I was the one who told the whole story about what went on between Alec and Trey. Back then I was trying to avoid trouble and now I was the center of it. After all, I did laugh at Tim along with everybody else, and I did repeat a bad name about him. Because I was a part of the joke, I just had to be honest.

"Yes, ma'am. It's true."

"I'm so surprised at you. You are one of our most prized students and until now your character has been **exceptional**. What happened?" said Dr. Sharpe.

"Oh, Morgan, what were you thinking?" Miss Nelson joined in, shaking her head. She wasn't pleased with me at all.

"Miss Love, since this is your fault, I want you to clean

up this mess and then come with me to my office. Do you understand, young lady?" Dr. Sharpe said.

All I could do was look at her and then bow my head. It hurt to hear kids from other classes that I didn't even know talking about me.

"Oooh, that's what she gets for laughin' at a special boy. Look at her, she's not so smart now," one girl said.

"We should throw more stuff down on the ground for her to pick up," said another girl.

"I wish you would throw more stuff down there," I heard Trey say.

Then he and Alec got down on the ground to help me. Was Alec my friend after all? I didn't even think he knew what the word help means.

When Mr. Brown, the custodian, brought over a broom and a waste basket, Chanté and Brooke also joined in and the five of us picked up all the smashed cups and the slushy mess.

"Morgan, can you believe this?" asked Brooke.

"Are you kiddin' me? We were just havin' fun. No one was tryin' to upset Tim. Now I gotta go to the office, Brooke. And I can't believe it. It's Field Day, and I gotta go to the office. I wasn't the only one who said it, but I'm not going to tell on someone else because I'm in trouble."

When we were finished cleaning, Dr. Sharpe told me to follow her.

Alec whispered, "You're gonna be okay, Morgan. Stay strong."

I nodded. Walking a little behind Dr. Sharpe, I prayed, *Lord, I'm so sorry. I guess this is what will happen when I join in on something that's wrong. I guess that's what Mom means when she tells me to think before I act and do something stupid. I didn't mean for that boy Tim to get upset. I just wanted to be cool like my friends, so I followed the crowd. And now I'm in big trouble. This is just great. Help me, please.*

On the way to the principal's office, I kept hearing sobbing in the hallway. Then as we got closer, I could tell it was Tim.

"I'm still trying to calm him down," a teacher's aide said to the principal.

"Are you happy about this, young lady?" Dr. Sharpe said, motioning for me to take a seat.

All I could do was hang my head down. I felt lower than an ant crawling on the ground. Tim was taken to another room, and I was left alone with Dr. Sharpe. I knew a long talk was coming, but I deserved it. I was wrong, and I needed whatever punishment she was going to give me.

"Morgan, you are a smart student. You pass all of your tests, and your grades are very good. Overall, you're a great student. However, you're only as good as the things you do. As quickly as you make a bad decision, your character can get ruined. Why would you pick on this young man? Clearly, you can see that he has a **disability.**"

Though she asked me a question, I didn't really think she wanted me to answer because she kept talking. I wanted to cry so badly, but I needed to be a big girl. I had gotten myself into this mess, and I had to take the punishment that came with it.

All I could think about was my classmates getting their ribbons, eating snow cones, and having lots of fun. But here I was sitting in the principal's office scared of what was going to happen to me.

It seemed like Dr. Sharpe had already talked to me for hours, but it had only been about five minutes. I knew that because I kept looking at the big clock on the wall. Thankfully, her phone rang, and she told the person on the line to "send them in."

Send them in? I thought. *Were the police here to take me away? Who is here? My folks! Oh, no!*

Even though I was in her office and in big trouble, it never dawned on me that she may have called my parents. But right away, I was relieved to see two people come in that I didn't even know. Then, as soon as they started talking with Dr. Sharpe, I knew they weren't happy at all.

"Morgan, these are Tim's parents, Mr. and Mrs. Clark," said Dr. Sharpe, motioning for them to have a seat.

Mrs. Clark began, "Hi, Morgan. We were just outside talking to your teacher, and she speaks highly of you. I know you probably got caught up in laughing at my son because he was getting picked on. At first, that probably didn't seem like a big deal. But this is the problem. My son is very intelligent and sensitive. And today you guys broke his heart. Even though he has a disability, he's come so far in trying to get out and enjoy life, but today I think you all set him back. I know you're young, sweetie, and you've got a lot to learn. We just want you to think twice before you make our son, or anyone else, the object of a cruel joke. Some people may seem different to you, but they're people just the same. They have feelings just like everyone else."

"Yes, ma'am," I said, unable to look at her. "I'm real sorry."

At that moment, I couldn't hold back the tears any longer. I hadn't only broken Tim's heart but obviously his parents were very hurt too. I never wanted to do any of that. It was a dumb thing to do, and maybe it was gonna be hard for me to pay the price. But somehow I was gonna make it up to them. I had to.

My back was to the door when they left so I didn't even see two other people walk in. But pretty soon I smelled Mom's perfume, and I felt Daddy Derek's strong presence. Without me even turning around, I knew it was them. I was shaking.

Mom didn't waste any time. "Morgan! Why were you sent to the principal's office? I had to get your dad from church, take Jayden to Mama's house, and rush over here because you were cutting up. Girl, you know I don't appreciate this, right?" she said, not paying any attention to my watery eyes.

"I just wanna hear it from her first," Daddy Derek spoke up. "Morgan, did you really pick on a child with special needs? That's hard for me to believe."

Mom cut in. "I love Morgan with all my heart, Derek.

And, yes, she's a very smart girl. But kids are kids and you can't just think that your kids are better than others. Everyone's child can make a mistake, including ours. They called us up here because she was laughing and joking along with her friends. The principal knows what she's talking about. Tell him, Morgan."

She was so upset with me. I could tell how much I'd let her down by the way she was talking.

I had never been in trouble at school. And I certainly didn't want to **inconvenience** anyone by having my parents go out of their way to get me. Now I was feeling worse than I already had been. When was this going to stop? I made a mistake. Okay? I feel bad about it. Okay? I learned my lesson. Okay?

It was time for me to tell how I felt, so I stood up and said, "I'm sorry! Yes, I did it. I didn't mean to hurt anybody. Yes, I was laughin' with the other kids, and I called Tim a bad name. I was just tryin' to be cool like my friends. I didn't want Tim to hear me. I understand that I let you down, Mom. And I'm so sorry!"

Mom just looked at me and said quietly, "You let yourself down, Morgan."

"Dr. Sharpe, what is her punishment?" Daddy Derek asked the principal.

"I don't want to suspend her with only one week left in school, but this behavior is unacceptable. She will have one day of in-school suspension."

I felt like I had swallowed a whole frog and it that was

31

jumping around in my throat. Suspension? In school? People were gonna walk by and see me through the glass doors with my back turned, doing tons of work. But doing extra work wasn't the thing that was getting to me. What would hurt the most was being away from my friends.

"How will this affect my child's school record?" asked Mom.

"It will be noted on her record that Morgan received an in-school suspension," Dr. Sharpe said. "But that will be a better outcome than giving her a home suspension."

I started to cry so hard that my head was hurting. I knew I was taking punishment for something I actually did. Yes, I laughed and called Tim that name, but someone else said it first. I just didn't think it was right for me to get another person in trouble. That girl should have admitted what she did.

Mom didn't even care how I was feeling. She said, "No need to cry now, honey. You should've thought about that before you made someone else cry. Laughing at someone and calling them harsh names is never a good choice. Now wipe those tears away and we'll deal with this when we get home."

Dr. Sharpe was writing out my suspension notice. Before she handed it to me, she said, "Morgan, you are a bright student. But you have to think about your actions before you do them. If you want to be a leader, you can't do something just because you see other people doing it. Always hold on to your high **morals** and good character. Do you understand?"

I nodded and tried to smile.

Then she made me wonder why she asked me, "Do you like sports?"

I nodded again.

Dr. Sharpe went on, "A football player wants to win the game and would never go out onto the field without wearing the proper equipment, right?"

"No, ma'am."

"That's correct. And if you want to be a winner, you can't go through school without the right equipment either. Having good character is part of the equipment you need to be a good person throughout your whole life."

"That's right, Morgan," Daddy Derek said, as he patted me on the back. "You can learn from this, honey."

They were right. I heard what they said, and I was going to have to remember it. I wished I could take back everything that went wrong, but that couldn't happen. Boy, was I going to be in for it when we got home.

• • • • •

As soon as we walked into the house, Mom didn't waste any time yelling. "Go to your room right now, until we decide on your punishment, young lady!"

I had never, ever seen my mom like this before. She was really angry with me. My parents' room was right next door to mine. Even with my head under the pillow, I could hear them arguing.

"This isn't like her," Daddy Derek said.

33

"It doesn't matter if it's like her or not. She did it, and now she has to take her punishment. I'm sick and tired of her acting out. We can't let her just get away with this."

"What do you mean 'sick and tired'? This is the first time we've had any problems out of Morgan," he said to her.

"She pouted all last summer and the first part of the school year. You never saw it because she was with her dad. But Derek, I've had enough. I can't let her get away with this kind of behavior. I must punish her."

Oh, my goodness. They were angry with me and now they were becoming angry with each other.

Then Daddy Derek said, "No, you don't have to do anything."

Thank you. Please talk her out of it, I thought in my head.

"I'm the man of the house, so that should be my job."

"What?" Mom said. "That's my daughter. I don't want you to discipline her."

"What do you mean? She's my daughter too, isn't she?"

Oh, no. This is not what should be happening. This is really bad. They were arguing over how to discipline me and the whole thing was my fault. Suddenly, their room door slammed and I got scared.

I got up and quietly shut my door. Then I fell onto my knees and prayed, *Oh Lord. I've done it this time. I've made a real big mess. I hope that Tim and his parents are okay. I want my parents to be okay. Help me, please.*

As I grow up, there will always be things in my life that will **tempt** me. So I'm gonna have to learn how to make smart decisions. I can't do something that I know is wrong just because everybody else is doing it. I know better than to follow people into a store and take some candy just to be cool, so why would I think it was okay to make someone feel bad? I didn't wanna hurt Tim's feelings. I did it because my friends thought it was cool.

Besides, it's not just about staying out of trouble. It's about doing the right thing. So it's better to do what Jesus would do rather than what my friends would do. And I know the Lord would never laugh at someone.

Just then the telephone rang and I saw on the caller ID that it was Brooke's number. I quickly picked it up.

"Hello?"

"Hey, it's me and Chanté. Can you talk?" Brooke was almost whispering.

"I'm sure I can't. My parents are arguing and mad, and I'm in big trouble," I whispered.

"Sorry about everything," Chanté said softly.

"It's not your fault. Tim heard me call him the name that everyone was laughin' about."

"I tried to tell you that he was right behind you," said Brooke.

"So what happened when you were in Dr. Sharpe's office?" Chanté asked.

"I got a one day suspension in school."

"Oh, that's not too bad," Brooke said. "It could've been worse."

"It's not so good either."

Brooke said, "Well, the whole class felt bad. Alec and Trey were talkin' about how they hoped you weren't in serious trouble. It's weird how you got them to be friends again."

"I know, right? Who would've thought?" Chanté added. "Well, anyway it's too bad that you won't be in class. You'll probably get bored being by yourself and everything."

"You don't have to make her feel bad about it," Brooke said.

"It's okay, I did it to myself. I'm findin' out that when you do the wrong thing, you have to take your punishment."

All of a sudden, my room door swung open. "Oh, no! Morgan, I know you're not on that telephone! When it didn't ring a second time, your mom and I thought the caller hung up. The last person in this house who needs to be talking on the phone is you. Hang that phone up, now!" Daddy Derek said, raising his voice.

"Bye, y'all," I quickly told them.

"I'm sorry, Morgan," Chanté said.

"Me too," Brooke said, before I hung up the phone.

"I can't believe this. I'm in there talking with your mom about what happened and here you are on the telephone acting like you're not in trouble. Do you think that it's okay to get an in-school suspension for making someone feel bad and then come home and everything will be the same? Well, that's about enough."

Uh, oh, I thought. *Here it comes.*

"There will be no television until we say so. You're going to get in there and learn how to do the dishes. If you're old enough to joke on people, then you're old enough to clean up the kitchen. And if you think you're so smart that you can talk on the phone while you're in trouble, then—"

I knew that for the rest of my life I'd think twice about everything I did. I didn't wanna make any more bad decisions because—trouble costs.

Letter to Dad

Dear Dad,

You won't believe this, Dad. I had to go to the principal's office today and give an **explanation**. She said I was an **exceptional** student, but that I was wrong for laughing at a student with a **disability**. I was wrong, Dad, and I feel horrible. It was an **inconvenience** to Mom and Daddy Derek because they had to come to the school and get me.

Dad, I can see you reading this, and I know I've let you down too. I do have **morals** and I know right from wrong. I wanted to fit in, and I laughed only so people would think I was cool. It was wrong for me to **tempt** other kids to be unkind too. Don't worry, I'm in big trouble. Mom and Daddy Derek were fussing about how they would **discipline** me. I messed up so bad that I have them arguing.

Dad, even though you may be mad at me, can I ask you to pray for your daughter? Please? I'll get it together soon. I need you here to help me. Come home, Dad.

Your daughter,
A lot to learn, Morgan

Word Search

```
E  M  E  X  I  S  T  R  I  J  S  M
E  X  C  E  P  T  I  O  N  A  L  U
D  B  P  F  L  A  S  H  C  Y  A  S
I  I  O  L  N  L  W  C  O  D  R  E
S  E  S  I  A  E  Q  A  N  E  O  U
A  X  T  C  B  N  U  R  V  N  M  M
B  C  P  O  I  T  A  D  E  Z  A  S
I  E  R  U  R  P  I  T  N  D  X  R
L  P  A  P  D  I  L  O  I  K  I  O
I  T  Y  O  N  A  L  I  E  O  M  E
T  E  M  P  T  R  A  J  N  L  N  K
Y  O  U  A  R  E  N  I  T  E  O  X
```

DISABILITY

DISCIPLINE

EXCEPTIONAL

EXPLANATION

INCONVENIENT

MORALS

TEMPT

Words to Know and Learn

1) **ex·pla·na·tion** (ĕk'splə-nā'shən) *noun*
The act or process of putting information into plain words

2) **ex·cep·tion·al** (ĭk-sĕp'shə-nəl) *adjective*
Well above average; something or someone who is special

3) **dis·a·bil·i·ty** (dĭs'ə-bĭl'ĭ-tē) *noun*
A physical or mental condition that prevents being able to do something

4) **in·con·ven·ience** (ĭn'kən-vēn'yəns) *noun*
A situation or something that is difficult or untimely that causes trouble

5) **mor·als** (môr'əl, mŏr'-) *noun*
Rules or habits of conduct that express standards of right and wrong

6) **dis·ci·pline** (dĭs'ə-plĭn) *verb*
To train according to rules or principles

7) **tempt** (tĕmpt) *verb*
To try to get (someone) to do wrong, especially by a promise of reward

Chapter 3

My Girl

"What are you doing?" Mom came into my bedroom. "We haven't agreed on Morgan's punishment. What's going on?"

Mom came over to comfort, me and I jumped right into her arms. Daddy Derek looked really upset. I was so scared. But I couldn't even **predict** the next thing that happened. It was something I didn't want to happen. The two of them started arguing really bad.

"Now wait one minute," Daddy Derek said to her. "Don't come in here yelling at me about disciplining Morgan. You don't even know what she was doing."

"Well, talk to me then. You don't need to go on about punishing my child," she said.

"Why do you keep saying that? She's my child too. Our child."

"Derek, we just talked about this. You know what I mean."

"I thought I did. I came in here to try and talk to her like we said we would. And she was in here on the phone . . . the phone!"

I knew I was in trouble now. Mom pushed me back from her just enough to look in my face. She stared at me hard and placed her hand on her hip. "Morgan, is this true? I know you weren't in here on the telephone, were you? You know you're on punishment, girl. What is the matter with you?"

I could imagine steam shooting from his ears when Daddy Derek continued making his case. "I walked in here and she's talking on the phone. She needs to understand what she did was wrong, and she's got to pay the price for her actions. In-school suspension? There's no way we can accept this."

"Yes, I understand that. But it's different coming from you. I'll handle it."

"You know what," Daddy Derek said. "Just forget it."

Then he left the room, slamming the door. What have I done? I didn't mean for them to be mad at each other. I was so sorry that all of this happened. I wanted to tell Daddy Derek to come back, but Mom wasn't in any mood to hear that. She paced back and forth across the floor, and I knew nothing I could say would make it better.

So I just sat on my bed and prayed silently. *Lord, this is not good. Now Mom and Daddy Derek aren't happy with each other. This reminds me of a few years ago when my parents weren't getting along, and it made me feel so bad. On the inside it felt like I had eaten something that tasted yucky, and I couldn't make it go away. Please make them better and not mad at each other.*

Then I got up and said, "Mommy, I'm gonna go and get Daddy Derek so he can discipline me. Is that okay?"

"Morgan, what are you talking about?"

"I don't want y'all to be mad at each other."

Then we heard a door open and close and a car took off from the driveway. Mommy looked at me.

"Oh no, he's gone!" I wailed.

"Baby, sometimes adults just need to be apart so that they won't blow up at each other. It's going to be all right. I'm really sorry that you had to see us argue. I really am. But that doesn't mean you're off the hook from what you did, Morgan. Maybe you didn't think that you would **disappoint** me by going against what was right. But you did. How could you think that being on the telephone is okay when you're on punishment? That's the last thing you need to do."

"I didn't mean . . . I think that . . . "

"No, Morgan, you were not thinking, and you need to start thinking, sweetie. You're almost in the third grade. You know right from wrong, and nothing was right about what you did. But Daddy Derek and I will be okay."

When she said that, her head hung low and then she walked out of my room. I felt even worse. As upset as Daddy Derek was when he left, I wasn't so sure that everything was gonna be okay. After all, Mom and Daddy's marriage didn't make it, so in my mind she and Daddy Derek might not make it either.

Jayden started crying and I heard Mom go into his room to take care of him and quiet him down. I wanted to make everything all better and I needed to, but I wasn't sure how. Then, it came to me! We hadn't eaten dinner yet, so I could help Mom that way. I didn't know how to cook, but I was gonna try my best to make some food for us.

I helped a lot of people in the kitchen. Mommy, Daddy Derek, Papa, and Mama. But I never tried anything on my own. Since I wasn't allowed to use the stove, I had to search high and low to find us something to eat. The only thing I saw that I could fix was some instant noodles.

My mom taught me how to break the noodles apart, add some water, and heat the bowl in the microwave. Then I had to use my school scissors and carefully cut off the top of the little packet to add the flavoring. It was easy, and it was yummy.

After I made her a bowl, I put it on the kitchen table and went into the nursery. "Mom, I fixed dinner for you," I said to her, before I saw she had tears in her eyes.

She laughed. "Oh, sweetie, you must be trying to make me feel better. What did you make me, a peanut butter and jelly sandwich?"

"I made you some of the noodles that you like."

"Okay, I'll be in there in just a second. It sounds perfect."

I walked back to the kitchen and heard a car pulling into the garage. I hurried to the door and peeked through the glass. When I saw Daddy Derek outside, I ran out to him.

"You're back! You didn't leave us!" I shouted.

He hugged me. "Morgan, I'm not going to leave you, Jayden, or your mom. I love you guys, and I'm sorry I lost my temper. The only reason I was going to discipline you is because I love you and I wanted to teach you a lesson."

"Yes, sir. I know. It's okay. You can punish me."

He just smiled and said, "Your mom and I need to decide on that first. But, don't ever think I'm going away. We're a family, and you're not ever going to lose me."

When we walked inside, Mom was standing in the doorway. She was holding the baby and more tears were falling from her eyes. He walked over to her and wiped them away. Then they hugged each other. God had heard my prayer.

"I love you," he said to her.

"I love you too. Are you hungry?"

"I'm starved."

"Morgan made us instant noodles."

They laughed. Then we all went to the kitchen and ate like a family should. Things were better. What a blessing.

• • • • •

It was Tuesday morning and the last week of school. I had already served my one day of in-school suspension. I was happy! I was excited! I was so glad to be back in Miss Nelson's classroom again. Everybody rushed up to me and said they were glad I was back.

Billy said to me, "Sorry you had in-school suspension. We all were joking at Tim and we all should've been in there with you."

"Yeah," Brooke said. "We just didn't wanna get in trouble too."

"I bet you really got it when you got home," Trey said. "I know when I got suspended, my parents . . . let's just say they weren't happy."

I didn't want to let everyone know what went on in my house about the whole punishment **ordeal**. That wasn't anything they needed to know. I was in trouble though. Big time! So I just shook my head.

Because it was the last week of school and we were done with all of our testing, Miss Nelson let us play games. They were educational games, of course, to help us review everything we learned in the second grade. Some kids played hangman to review the vocabulary words we learned all year. Others played a game to review math problems. The computer games had some students going on the loudest. The class was having a blast.

While people were in different groups playing, I walked over to my teacher's desk. "Miss Nelson, it's really, really bothering me that I made fun of Tim. I want to make it right. Can you help me come up with a way to apologize to him?"

She stood up from her desk and held both of my hands. "Morgan, you were the last person I thought would pick on Tim. You've been such a good student all year. I don't know what went wrong. I remember when you used to sit alone because kids were making fun of you. I just didn't understand why you would make someone else feel bad."

"I didn't even know he heard me. I really didn't want to make him feel bad. Honest."

"Coming to me and wanting to apologize for upsetting Tim is the Morgan Love I know. I'm so proud of you. You don't need me to help you figure out how to apologize. Just speak from your heart."

So I went over to my desk and sat there, staring at the sky through the classroom window. *Lord, what can I do so Tim will know that I'm sorry? What can I say? What would he like to hear?*

Then it came to me. The class could throw him a party! Miss Nelson helped me call my mom. I told her my idea and that I needed her help.

"Did your teacher say that it's okay for you to bring a cake?" Mom asked.

"Yes, but it has to be a store-bought one because they don't allow homemade foods in school, remember?"

"Yes, Morgan, I remember. And you want it to say: 'You're Amazing, Tim'?"

"Yes, ma'am. You've got it!"

"Okay, well I'll have it there in an hour," Mom said in a sweet and **pleasant** tone.

47

"Oh! And, Mom, can you bring some balloons too?"

"Well then, I'll be there in about an hour and fifteen minutes."

"Thanks, see you then!"

Miss Nelson sent me to the teacher's workroom to get a long piece of white paper. I felt so important, sort of like a teacher myself. After I got the size that I needed, I jetted back to the classroom. Then she said it was okay for me to speak to the class.

"Okay, everybody. I know you guys are all playin' games, but I need you to listen up. I want us to throw a party for Tim. Now we all owe him an apology, and we need to let him know how sorry we are."

Holding up the long, white paper, I said, "We're gonna make a special banner for him with this paper. If you have some nice words to say to him, you can write them on here."

All of a sudden everybody rushed to grab a crayon, marker, or colored pencil. Miss Nelson and I watched as they filled in the banner with wonderful notes and cute pictures. I couldn't wait for Tim to see it.

"I'll be right back, class. I want everyone to be on their best behavior until I return," Miss Nelson said before stepping out of the room.

When she came back, the banner was full of even more nice words, hearts, and smiley faces for Tim. "Oh, you guys. This is great. I just spoke with Tim's teacher, and he's at lunch. As soon as his lunch period is over, we can have our party! Dr. Sharpe says she can attend too."

I didn't even know that Miss Nelson was going to invite the principal, but it was cool. Thirty minutes later when Tim walked into the classroom and saw the cake and balloons and people clapping for him, he screamed. It wasn't a bad scream like on Field Day but a scream of happiness. His teacher told him that I organized the party and he came to shake my hand. I hugged him, and he cheered like I did something good.

While the class was eating cake, Mom came over to me and said, "Morgan, you are amazing. You definitely take lemons and make lemonade. What made you wanna do this?"

"Because we're all special, and I wanted to make this a special day for Tim to remember. I never want him to have another bad memory like he had the week before. He's an awesome kid, and he should feel good about himself."

"Ditto for you, young lady. You are amazing too. My Morgan."

Her kiss on the cheek made me happy. But I was even happier because it felt good to do something nice for someone else.

● ● ● ● ●

It was the weekend, and second grade was over. I was gonna miss my teacher and my friends. But summer was here, and it was time for me to enjoy it. That was going to be a little harder to do since Mom and Daddy Derek weren't talking that much. There was still some trouble between them. The whole thing about the right kind of discipline for me was not settled yet.

They didn't want me to hear them talking alone anymore, but I could tell something wasn't right. When Mom came into a room, Daddy Derek would leave the room. He'd watch TV upstairs, and she'd be downstairs. They weren't even playing with the baby together. Yep, something was wrong, and I wanted to know what it was.

I kept thinking really hard. They had eaten my instant noodles, and we had a nice quiet time. Ever since that day I've been trying hard to bring them together. But we still needed more peace in the house. And since Mommy liked the party I threw for Tim, maybe having one would make things better at home too.

The problem was I needed some help. I asked Mom if I could call my grandparents since I wasn't supposed to be talking on the phone. I didn't need to get in trouble again. When she agreed, I started to put my plan in **motion**.

Mama said, "So let me get this straight. You want me to cook dinner for them and bring it over to your house? Then take you and the baby so they can have a special time?"

"Yes, ma'am."

"Well, I've got to think about this," she said.

But Papa didn't **hesitate**.

"What's there to think about?" I heard Papa say in the background. "What time should we go over there?"

"Six o'clock. Okay?" I said, smiling from cheek to cheek.

"Sarah, you should be ashamed of yourself for giving that girl a hard time."

"Well, I need help making this meal so quickly. You be ready, young lady, I'm comin' to pick you up now," my grandmother said.

"But, Mama, you can't tell them what we're doing!"

"It's okay; I can keep a secret. Let me talk to your mom."

• • • • •

What an amazing meal we prepared! We made Cornish hens with steamed potatoes and broccoli. Mama also baked her homemade apple pie.

When we got back to my house, Daddy Derek wasn't there.

"What if he's not comin' home right away?"

"Don't worry, angel. It'll work out. Let's just get this set up," Papa said. "You work on your part, and I'll work on mine. We can't worry about what we can't control. This is a life lesson for you. Don't stress."

Mom was sleeping and so was the baby. We made sure to be quiet so we wouldn't wake them up.

Papa brought out his music player and Mama set the dining room table. She brought red roses from her garden as a **centerpiece**. And I wrote a nice note: *Dinner for two people whom I love and pray love each other. Sorry about everything. Love, Morgan*

When everything was ready, my grandmother woke up

my mom and asked if she could take me and Jayden back home with her for a while. Mom was glad to take a break so we packed up the baby and headed out.

Papa put on a video so we could watch a movie, but I couldn't concentrate because I was hoping my parents were enjoying their meal.

Two hours later, we arrived back at home and everything was quiet. All I could hear was the soft music Papa had turned on before we left. I rushed to the living room and found my parents dancing.

They opened their arms and asked me to join them. As the three of us twirled around, I knew everything was much better. They were smiling, and they were happy.

Daddy Derek said, "Your mom told me what a great party you threw for Tim. I thought that was something special. Morgan, this dinner you planned for your mom and me really touches my heart. I told you I wasn't going anywhere, but I realize you've been watching my actions. And I know they speak louder than words."

Mom added, "And we're going to make sure we talk with each other more. Thank you, Morgan, for caring. I know you feel our issue had been about you, but it was really about us. So we've decided we will both give you a punishment if you ever need it. We are one family and . . . "

All of a sudden, Daddy Derek let go of Mom's hand and twirled me by myself. "We both expect great things out of you. And just like you're her number one girl, never forget I love you too, and you're also my girl."

Letter to Dad

Dear Dad,

I told you I got in trouble at school, but I could never **predict** that I'd cause more trouble at home. I didn't mean to **disappoint** Mom and Daddy Derek. Through the whole bad **ordeal** they were arguing about how to deal with me. Then, I talked on the phone. I wasn't thinking that because I was on punishment I wasn't supposed to use it. So when they caught me, it wasn't **pleasant**.

After that, I didn't **hesitate**. I wanted to fix everything I messed up. I set a plan in **motion** to make things better. I had a party for the special needs boy, Tim. And, Dad, he loved it. Then I arranged a special dinner for Mom and Daddy Derek. Mama and I decorated the dining room to look like a fancy restaurant. The **centerpiece** full of fresh roses was really pretty. The sad mood they were in was lifted. So now my life is better. Miss you, Dad.

> Your daughter,
> Much more caring, Morgan

Word Search

```
M  C  D  O  N  A  L  B  U  R  G  R
O  C  O  P  P  L  E  A  S  A  N  T
R  D  E  E  U  Z  M  S  A  N  C  N
G  R  S  N  N  K  O  E  J  I  B  I
A  N  O  I  T  O  M  B  D  W  A  O
N  L  P  Q  O  E  O  E  I  C  R  P
N  I  H  T  R  Y  R  F  N  O  N  P
O  S  H  E  E  P  N  P  V  R  E  A
E  E  R  I  X  D  A  V  I  D  Y  S
L  H  H  E  S  I  T  A  T  E  V  I
L  E  K  I  N  G  Q  U  E  A  C  D
E  S  I  T  A  T  E  A  P  L  L  E
```

CENTERPIECE

DISAPPOINT

HESITATE

MOTION

PLEASANT

PREDICT

ORDEAL

Words to Know and Learn

1) **pre·dict** (prĭ-dĭkt') *verb*
To guess ahead of time that something will happen

2) **dis·ap·point** (dĭs'ə-point') *verb*
To fail to satisfy the hope, desire, or expectation of someone

3) **or·deal** (ôr-dēl') *noun*
A hard thing to go through

4) **pleas·ant** (plĕz'ənt) *adjective*
Pleasing in manner, behavior, or appearance

5) **mo·tion** (mō'shən) *noun*
The act or process of changing a position or place

6) **cen·ter·piece** (sĕn'tər-pēs') *noun*
An arrangement, usually flowers, placed at the center of a table

7) **hes·i·tate** (hĕz'ĭ-tāt') *verb*
To be slow to act, speak, or decide on something

Chapter 4

Double Take

Summer was here. Yea! But my cousins were coming over. Boo! It wasn't that I had a problem with Samantha (who liked to be called Sam), Drake, and Sadie. We had worked out all of our issues when they visited over the Christmas holiday last year.

But, I didn't like sharing my room, and I didn't like the idea of not having as many snacks around when I wanted them. Having a lot of people in the house makes the food go quickly. Since I didn't have any other choice, I had to deal with it. I promised myself that I was gonna try and have a good attitude.

Surprisingly, everyone was in their own world. Drake was downstairs playing video games. I was in the family room reading my books. Sadie asked my mom if she could play with the baby. I liked playing with him too, but I lived with Jayden and for me it was the same old thing.

Sadie got a kick out of helping, and my mom liked the extra help. Sam was in the bathroom, as always, combing her hair most of the day. Every time someone wanted to use it, we had to knock on the door and ask her. Then she would take forever to come out. As soon as one person finished, Sam was back in the bathroom with the door locked again.

At dinner, Daddy Derek asked us what we did today. We all pretty much said the same thing—nothing. Summer had just started, and it was already boring. My cousins were gonna stay with us during the week because Mom was home during the day. Their mom got a new job working nights and needed someone to watch them. But they would be going home on the weekends.

"Uncle Derek, can you take us to Six Flags?" Drake asked.

"Or to the zoo," said Sadie.

"I just wanna go to the mall sometimes," Sam added.

Honestly, I just wanted them to go home.

"We might take a trip or two this summer, but you guys need to be more creative with your ideas. Think outside the **typical** things you want to do. Summer fun can be more than going to the amusement park and going swimming."

"What do you mean?" Drake asked, sucking down Mom's spaghetti. Sauce was dripping all over his face, and he took the next bite without even wiping his mouth. I couldn't help but think, *Boys. Ugh and yuck!* Enough said.

Daddy Derek continued, after he motioned for Drake to

use his napkin. "Well, when I was your age, I used to explore nature. I knew how to get out there and have fun. All last month I was in the backyard clearing out a path that leads to the creek."

"Derek, those kids don't need to be out there playing around the creek," Mommy said.

"They can't actually get to the creek because there's a fence blocking anyone from getting to it. It's the summer. You guys should be kids and go create some excitement. Explore."

"I won't be doing that, Uncle Derek," Sam stood up and said. "May I be excused?"

He looked at her plate. The salad was still there and so was the pile of spaghetti and a whole piece of garlic bread. Sam had barely touched her dinner and she was ready to leave the table. Even her water glass was full.

"No, you can't be excused, girl. There's still food on your plate. Sit down and eat something," he told her.

"I just can't believe how much you've grown," Mom said to Sam. "You're such a cute size . . . just a little lady."

Sam scared me when she snapped back, "I'm not little!"

Daddy Derek gave her a tough stare. Even her brother and sister looked at her like she was trippin'.

"I'm sorry," she said quickly.

I didn't know what was up with her and I didn't care. She was so moody. When she first walked through the door, I had to take a double look myself. Sam didn't look like the same girl who stayed at our house over Christmas break.

I really wanted to ask her what she does in the bathroom so long. But my mouth was full of delicious spaghetti! Mom told me never to talk with my mouth full. Sam seemed **reluctant,** but she sat back down. I could tell she wasn't going to be opening up to anyone anytime soon.

"Uncle Derek, I don't like outdoors," Sadie said. "There are too many bugs. Even more bugs. And a whole lot more bugs. Yuck!"

"Sadie, it's not that bad. You're young, and this is the perfect time for you to discover the outdoors. You just might find out there's more to life than Barbie dolls and video games."

"Ooohh, can I take the baby out there?" Sadie's face looked happy like she just got a great idea.

Both Mom and Daddy Derek looked at each other and said, "No!" at the same time. Drake and I just laughed.

"So, Morgan, you wanna go and check it out?" Drake asked me.

Was he talking to me? We had never hung out before. Why was he asking me now? I never even thought about running around in the woods. But, the more I thought about it, maybe it would be cool.

I finished chewing my food. Then I said, "I've never been back there, but Daddy Derek thinks we should try it. Wanna go tomorrow?"

"Derek, are you sure it's okay for the kids to go? It's so far away," Mom asked him. She was always worrying about everything.

"Yeah, Uncle Derek, are you sure it's good for us to be back there?" Sadie asked.

"Well, it is a pretty big space. I'll walk around with them in the morning to make sure it's safe. These kids need some adventure rather than sitting around the house whining about being bored."

Then he told us kids, "When you use your imagination to dream and explore, you can go all over the world. You could discover places that you never knew existed."

Drake, Sadie, and I had no idea what he was talking about. But we knew we had to be up early enough to take the walk with him in the morning.

Daddy Derek was in a teaching mood, and he wasn't finished yet. While we finished eating our meal, he used the time to find out what we were thinking about.

"So, how are you all planning to spend your summer?" Daddy Derek asked us.

"I plan to relax and do no work, that's for sure," Drake said very proudly.

"Drake, around here you will enjoy yourself, and you will also do work. The summer is a chance to rest, but to also get ahead of what's next."

None of us looked happy to hear him pushing us.

"For example, instead of always watching funny TV shows, you should tune in to the History Channel, the

Discovery Channel, or a PBS station to watch some educational programs. That kind of TV watching will **expand** your mind. Yep, I've made a decision. We're going to enjoy this summer by learning. There'll be no sitting around and letting it waste away."

● ● ● ● ●

The next morning at nine o'clock sharp, Drake, Sadie, and I were up and ready to explore. Sam wasn't going with us so she stayed in bed. Mommy watched us as we headed out the back door and into the backyard. Daddy Derek led the way.

"Okay, let's go," he said.

He had given each of us a backpack filled with goodies. And Mom had laid out some things for us too. I reached for a blanket. Drake grabbed the water jug. And Sadie picked up the flashlight.

"What are you gonna do with that?" Drake asked, trying to snatch it away from her.

"You never know. We might need it."

"It's daytime, sis."

We ended up leaving the flashlight behind and were off for adventure. The area behind the yard was really big like Daddy Derek said it was. He pointed out different spots along our **journey.**

"See, this space that I cut away connects to the walking trail that the city takes care of. I only want you guys to come this far, so don't go any farther. Morgan, I'm sure your mom will be looking for you in two hours to come in the house. Okay?"

I nodded.

"Drake, you have your cell phone. We'll call if we need you before then."

"Yes, sir," Drake responded, saluting his hand like a soldier as Daddy Derek turned to go back.

On one side of the path was a little open area. It was just the right size for us to lay down our blanket. We just sat there, looking up at the sky.

Everybody was quiet until Drake spoke first. "What do you do out here in the woods? Maybe I could climb a tree."

"So how do you think you'll feel when you fall down and break your leg?" asked Sadie.

Drake thought for a moment and said, "Okay, then. Maybe I'll climb that fence and go for a swim."

"No, you're not climbing a fence and getting into the creek. I heard Daddy Derek say there are cameras out here. First of all, you could go to jail. Second of all, you could get hurt. And third of all, you wouldn't be able to sit down for a month from the spanking you'd get," I warned him.

"True, true, and true. Then . . . what *are* we gonna do out here?" Drake asked again.

"He said to use our imagination," I reminded him.

"We could tell scary stories," Sadie suggested.

"Say what now?" Drake asked.

"I could start us out," Sadie said.

"No, Sadie, be quiet," Drake told her.

Sadie squinted her eyes. "Whatever. Hey, do you hear that noise?"

"What noise, girl?"

"Over there," she said, pointing in one direction. It's like the pitter patter of little feet. It's a chipmunk, a pink chipmunk. Don't you see it?"

"What are you talkin' about, Sadie? Stop playing games."

"Shhh! You're messin' up my story. In Dream Land, there lived the chipmunk family. One chipmunk is named Bright. They called her Bright because she wasn't brown like everyone else. She was bright pink. Even though she was the prettiest chipmunk you'd ever seen, she didn't like herself. She wanted to be like all the other chipmunks and not stand out. So when everyone was asleep one night, she left her chipmunk family in Dream Land.

"Bright went all the way to Dreadful Land. She just wanted to be by herself and think about her life. But she had no idea that Dreadful Land had a mean snake family that was waiting to capture any chipmunk they could find. She only knew she wanted to get away from her family and not embarrass them anymore because she was so different."

"Oooh, oooh! I see her!" I said. I was getting excited about where the story could go.

"You do not," Drake said, giving me a weird look.

"I do too. Hi, Bright!"

"Hi," the scared little pink chipmunk said to me. "Should I talk to them?" She asked the big oak tree standing right behind her.

Drake cut in, acting like the oak tree. He couldn't help but join the fun.

"And then, all of a sudden, the tree came alive and told Bright, 'Yes. They're good kids. You can talk to them,'"

"So, Bright, why did you run away?" I pretended to ask the imaginary chipmunk.

In my head, I could picture the pretty, pink chipmunk standing right in front us.

"I just wanna go home. I ran away too far and the snake family is after me," said Sadie.

"How did the snake family know you were here?"

"The flies told them."

The three of us walked over to a big tree. We circled the tree and found a little hole on one side of it.

"Mr. Oak Tree, is there a place where we could protect Bright?"

"Sure. But you have to work quickly if you wanna keep Bright safe," Drake said.

We were having so much fun with the story. So we worked together to dig a deeper hole for Bright to live in. We danced with Bright and we cheered with Bright. Drake even pretended to play ball with Bright. It was so cool that we even made up a chipmunk language. We all pressed on our noses and stuck out our teeth trying to be like chipmunks.

We were having a blast and then Drake's cell phone rang.

I pretended like Bright got scared and jumped into my arms.

"You're a good person, Morgan. I was frightened before I met you guys, but you made me feel safe. I know you're not supposed to run away from your problems. But with your help, I know I'll make it back home. Can you help me?" Bright looked very pitiful.

Breaking up our playtime, Drake said, "Guys, we gotta go. Uncle Derek said we should have been home by now."

We tucked Bright into her little hole. Then we closed her in with twigs and leaves so the snake family couldn't find her. We made a pact with Bright that we would visit her tomorrow. And the three of us giggled all the way home. Using our imagination was so much fun. We all agreed that the day had been a successful one.

• • • • •

As soon as we got close to the house, Daddy Derek was standing at the back door. He didn't have the happiest look on his face, but the three of us were so busy being happy that we didn't even notice. We had laughed so hard all the way home from Dream Land.

When we started to run as fast as we could to reach Daddy Derek, Sadie's face changed.

"Uh oh. We're in trouble."

"Nuh uh. He wanted us to have fun and that's what we did. Let me handle this," Drake said, taking charge.

Drake thought just because he and Daddy Derek were close that he could get us out of trouble. Sadly, that wasn't the case this time.

But he tried anyway. He walked up to Daddy Derek like he was a grown-up or something.

"What's up, Unc?" he said in his cool voice.

"Boy, get your silly self in this house. I told you guys to be back here in two hours and that time passed a long time ago. You just forget about that, right? My wife is sitting in there worried about you. We didn't know what was going on. You didn't stay on the path like I told you. When I came looking for you, you were nowhere to be found. Drake, thank goodness you had your cell phone or we would've thought someone had snatched you guys."

The three of us looked at each other like we were about to get it now. Daddy Derek told us not to **venture** off the path, but that's what we had done. We were so busy playing in Dream Land. I guess time sure does fly when you're having fun. Even though he had told us to enjoy ourselves, now we were gonna have to pay big time for our fun. Grown-ups can sometimes be so confusing.

"Wait, we have to tell you all about what we did, Uncle Derek," Sadie said.

"Not now," Daddy Derek said. "Get in the house and wash up. Lunch is on the table."

I skipped on in the house and saw Mom setting the table. "Mom, we had such a great time today! Playing with my cousins was better than Field Day."

"Morgan, do I look like someone who wants to hear that right now? You all had me worried sick, girl."

"I'm sorry, Mommy," I said, trying to give her a hug. But she stepped away.

"I know you're growing up, and you're excited about the fun you're having with your cousins, but there are some places that you can't go to by yourself. That's why we set rules and **boundaries** for you guys. Don't get so caught up with listening to other people that you forget who you're supposed to listen to. Do you understand me?"

"Yes, ma'am," I said, with a long face.

"Now go and get washed up," she said when she smacked my bottom playfully.

I skipped some more down the hallway to see Sadie knocking on the bathroom door. I had been talking to Mommy long enough for her to be finished washing up for lunch by now.

"You haven't gone in yet?" I asked her.

"My sister's in there."

"She's always in there," I said, as I started banging on the door. "Sam, we have to get in the bathroom!"

She finally came out. Her eyes were watery, and she looked really tired. That didn't make sense because she hadn't gone anywhere or done anything. It wasn't like she'd been running around outside like the rest of us. So, why was she so tired?

Ten minutes later, we were all seated at the dining room table. We had to sit in there because the kitchen table wasn't big enough for everyone. No one said a word. The sounds of forks and spoons hitting the plates were all we heard.

"All right, I'm not gonna sit at this table with these long faces. Talk me to. Tell me all about this great day that got you all off your trail," Daddy Derek said, finally breaking the ice.

The three of us couldn't wait to spill the beans and tell him about our make-believe land. We were all trying to talk at the same time. Mom, Sam, and Daddy Derek all looked confused.

Finally, Daddy Derek said, "Wait a minute! We can't hear you all at once. One at a time, please."

"Okay, I'll go first," Drake said right away. "See, we went to this faraway land."

Sadie added, "We met this pink chipmunk that needed our help. Her name is Bright."

"Yep, the lime green snakes were trying to get her," I said.

"We put her in a safe place and told her we'll be back tomorrow."

"It's really not that far from where you told us to go," Drake said.

Daddy Derek said, "I'll have to check it out."

"Ugh! Can I be excused?" Sam asked, as if we were boring her.

"But sweetheart, you haven't eaten your meal," my mom said to her.

She huffed and took three huge bites. Her mouth couldn't even **contain** all she stuffed inside it.

"What's wrong with you anyway?" Drake asked. "It

69

looked like you were cryin' when you came out of the bathroom."

Barely able to speak as she tried to keep all the food in her mouth, she mumbled, "Nothing's wrong with me. Okay? Can I go now?"

Mom looked at Daddy Derek and then told Sam to eat some more bites. She did, but she didn't like it. When she got up and left, the three of us were ready to finish our story. We had to repeat some parts because we kept leaving out stuff. I could tell that Mom and Daddy Derek were listening to every word.

"So, can we go back tomorrow? We can't add more to the story unless we go back," said Drake.

"Like I said, I'll go out with you all in the morning. But, again, you'll have a certain time to be back. And if I don't think it's safe enough for you guys, then you're coming back with me. Cool?"

"Yes, sir!" we all said together.

The rest of the day was going okay. Sadie and I played with the baby for a while and Drake played his video game. Sam was upstairs. Most likely she was doing her usual thing, standing in front of the mirror and brushing her hair.

Drake and Sadie both decided at the same time that they wanted to watch TV before it was time for bed. So they rushed downstairs to see who could get the remote first. That was okay with me because I had to go to the bathroom anyway. The door was cracked, and I didn't think anyone was in there. But I walked in to find a big surprise. Sam was leaning over the toilet with her hand in her mouth. I couldn't believe what I was seeing and did a double take.

Letter to Dad

Dear Dad,

Summer is finally here, and I'm glad it didn't start with a **typical** kind of day. My cousins are staying with us again, and we've been on an adventure. Daddy Derek encouraged us to play outdoors. At first we were **reluctant** to go exploring in the back-yard. But it was good that we got the chance to **expand** our minds and play in the woods.

The **journey** was so much fun. The trail is clear and kept by the city, so it's safe. But Daddy Derek told us not to **venture** off too far. We were given **boundaries** but were having too much fun and went off doing other things. That got us into trouble. Don't worry, we'll **contain** ourselves the next time and stay on course.

I thought about you when I was out there. You do so much for our country, and I love you for it. I pray I'll see you soon.

Your daughter,
Explorer Morgan

Word Search

```
M  P  B  O  U  N  D  E  D  U  S  A
B  O  U  N  D  A  R  I  E  S  D  M
O  R  C  E  X  J  K  I  L  N  N  E
U  C  O  X  V  O  F  L  A  B  A  R
N  O  A  P  E  U  O  P  C  R  V  I
D  N  C  A  N  R  X  Y  I  O  A  C
I  T  H  N  T  E  A  M  P  O  L  A
N  A  J  O  U  R  N  E  Y  K  O  N
G  I  O  W  R  C  R  T  T  E  V  E
V  N  A  U  E  A  D  M  I  R  A  L
E  Z  K  R  E  L  U  C  T  A  N  T
N  T  U  R  E  M  O  R  G  A  N  L
```

CONTAIN

BOUNDARIES

EXPAND

JOURNEY

RELUCTANT

TYPICAL

VENTURE

Words to Know and Learn

1) **typ·i·cal** (tĭp'ĭ-kəl) *adjective*
Having the qualities, traits, or characteristics of a particular group or category

2) **re·luc·tant** (rĭ-lŭk'tənt) *adjective*
Unwilling or not enthusiastic

3) **ex·pand** (ĭk-spănd') *verb*
To increase the size, volume, quantity, or scope of; enlarge

4) **jour·ney** (jûr'nē) *noun*
The act of traveling from one place to another

5) **ven·ture** (věn'chər) *verb*
To move, travel, or go in a brave or daring manner

6) **bound·a·ries** (boun'də-rē, -drē) *noun* (plural)
Something that indicates a border or limit

7) **con·tain** (kən-tān') *verb*
To hold back; set limits on; also, to have within

Chapter 5

Keeping Secrets

I couldn't believe what I was seeing! My cousin Sam was trying not to keep her food down on **purpose**. Why would she do that?

"What are you doing?" I asked, gasping.

I scared her, and she jerked up from the floor. Sam quickly flushed the toilet. It wasn't like I wanted to see what was in there anyway. She was straightening her clothes and wiping her mouth at the same time. Trying to explain, she was saying more than I've heard her say the whole time she's been here.

"You didn't see anything, Morgan. Okay? Just forget this. Please? Please don't say anything. It's no big deal."

"There's still stuff all over your mouth," I said, as I looked away. "I don't understand, Sam. Why don't you want to keep your food down? Why were your fingers in your mouth? What's going on?"

She began to cry as she went over to the sink and grabbed her face towel. I knew she wanted me to just go away and not say anything about what I'd seen. But that wasn't gonna happen. She had to talk to me if she wanted me to be quiet about this. I needed to understand.

So I stood there with my hands on my hips like I was my mom and said, "Explain."

Sam started crying harder and, of course, I felt bad. The toilet seat was down so I went over and sat on it. I was waiting for her to calm herself, dry her face, and talk to me.

"You just don't get it, Morgan. I'm in middle school now, and once you get there everything changes. The last couple of weeks have been **miserable** for me. My friends started callin' me fat. I couldn't fit into my regular shirts because my tummy has gotten bigger. The boys started checkin' out other girls and none of them would even look at me. You probably think boys are gross now, but when you get to be my age you don't want them to think you're not the one who's cool."

Huh? I thought. I heard everything she was saying and I was trying to take it all in. But I was confused. I could tell this must mean a lot to her because Sam was making such a big deal over it. But, from what I saw of her small body, she was just trippin' because she surely wasn't fat!

"Sam, you're not fat," I told her.

"You don't know anything! I am so fat!" Her words were loud enough for the whole house to hear.

"I'm not gonna have to keep anything a secret much longer. As loud as you're talkin', everyone will be in here any minute."

Sam knew I was right. She walked over to me with her finger in front of her lips. "Gosh, you're right. Morgan, please don't say anything."

"You're much older than me, Samantha, and you're about the same size as me, just taller. How can you say you're big?"

"I wish you could understand, but you don't. A lot is goin' on with my body that you'll know about later on. Right now, you can eat everything in the world. When your mom cooks, she and Uncle Derek make you eat everything on your plate. But my body can't take it. A girl has to be happy with herself, and that means she's gotta look good."

"But that starts on the inside. That's what Mama tells me. That's what Papa tells me too. That's what my mom, my dad, and even Daddy Derek tell me. If you've got the Lord in your heart, then you can feel good about who you are. Who cares what other people think?"

"Well, maybe that's true, Morgan. But I don't wanna be a big, fat pig. I know that fat can creep up on you. That's why I couldn't eat all that spaghetti yesterday. And I couldn't eat that hamburger and French fries today. Before you know it, I could gain twenty pounds! You see, I don't have two parents at home like you do."

"What does that have to do with anything?" I asked her.

"My mom struggles to pay the bills, and she can't afford to buy me more clothes if I gain weight. It's hard for her to buy any clothes for that matter. You remember last Christmas when you got everything?"

Boy, I sure didn't want her to bring up the whole Christmas thing again. I did get everything plus some more. And she, her brother, and sister barely got anything at all. We all learned that Christmas wasn't about **monetary** gifts, but it did hurt their feelings that they had so much less.

"I remember."

"So you see, when I go to school I don't look as cute as a lot of people wearing their new clothes. That's why I have to have a great shape. Besides, I want to lose weight to make the track team this year. So, just don't say anything, Morgan. I know what I'm doing," Sam said, getting a little snippy.

"But it looks like you're hurting yourself. It can't be healthy to act that way."

"I just don't need to keep down my food. That's all."

"I need to talk to my mom about this," I said and got up to leave.

Sam quickly stepped in front of me and blocked the door. "You're not goin' anywhere until you promise not to say a word."

"My mom told me there are some things I'm supposed to tell. I got in trouble for something like this before at school. And I'm not gonna let you keep hurting yourself."

"But I'm not hurting myself!"

"Is everything okay in there?" Mom finally came to the door and asked.

It was the moment of truth. Sam looked at me with puppy dog eyes, all sad and pitiful. She needed me to assure her that I was gonna keep quiet about what I saw.

Right away, I thought, *What would Jesus do?* This was a huge decision. I decided to keep quiet—but just for now.

I opened up the door and said, "Everything is okay, Mom."

Sam smiled and gave me a big hug. I smiled back. But, I really hoped she would stop hurting herself so everything would be okay with her. I knew I'd have to watch her, though. If something happened to her, I don't know what I'd do.

• • • • •

"I'm so glad you came to my party," Brooke said to me, when I arrived at her birthday bash. Her mother had set up the backyard with pretty pink and white balloons. It looked like it was going to be a great time.

We had just come from a picnic at church, so Mom dropped me off a little late. When I looked around, just about everybody from our class was there. They all rushed up to greet me. Everyone, except Alec. I didn't know if Brooke didn't invite him because she still didn't like him too much, or if she tried to invite him and found out he was out of town visiting his grandparents. Anyway, I was glad to see Trey and Chanté too.

"Come here, come here. I have to tell you a secret," Brooke said, yanking on my arm.

I barely got a chance to speak to all of my friends and classmates before she was pulling me inside the house. I wanted to know what she had to tell me, but I wanted to eat and greet too. I didn't eat at the picnic because I knew I was coming to her party. Also, I missed my friends, and I was ready to play some games with them.

"Brooke, I'm hungry. Hurry up and tell me," I said when she was taking so long to get her news out.

"Okay, it's really quick . . . no, on second thought . . . I don't think I'm gonna tell you because you can't keep a secret, and it'll be a big mess."

"What are you talking about?"

She was acting so **thrilled** that it really made me want to know what was going on. Something about her had changed but I didn't know what it was. Maybe she was just excited because it was her party, but something was making her act nervous and kind of different.

"Girl, just tell me."

"You ready?"

"Yes, tell me!"

She came closer and whispered in my ear, "Trey came up to me and told me I look pretty today."

"Well, if he actually said it, then he already knows. How can it be a secret?"

"Because I don't want anybody else to know, so don't

say anything. He called me pretty!" She grinned, jumping up and down.

We went back outside to join the others. Though I wasn't going to say anything about Trey thinking Brooke was cute, I did notice he kept staring at her and smiling. I went over to the table to get a hamburger and some chips.

Trey walked up to me and said, "Hey, Morgan. I'm glad you're here."

A part of me wanted him to tell me I looked nice today, but he didn't. He just asked me to be on his team for kickball. Not even giving him an answer, I just plopped ketchup on my food and moved away. I was bummed out and didn't understand why. In the second grade, the girls in my class didn't get along so great with the boys. It was pretty great that we ended the year on a good note. I stopped Trey from hurting Alec really bad when I told Miss Nelson about their fight. I mean, they got in trouble but it could've been much worse.

Deep down inside I wanted to be pretty too, but Trey didn't see me that way. When I looked over at the birthday girl with her long hair in pretty curls, wearing that cute sundress, I knew she wasn't about to play kickball. Then here I was with my shorts, T-shirt, and tennis shoes, ready to take on any boy who thought they could beat me.

I was confused and unhappy. Maybe I wanted to be a different Morgan. Maybe I wanted to get rid of my boyish look. I didn't like how I was feeling. It was like I was jealous of my best buddy, and that wasn't right.

When it was time to cut the cake, all the boys were crowding around Brooke. Chanté was sitting by herself, and I went to join her.

"Those boys are crazy, right?" Chanté said and laughed.

"What do you mean?"

"All day they've been trying to be in Brooke's face. I hope I look that cute on my birthday."

"Who cares if boys think you're cute?" I said, even though deep down I had to make myself feel like that wasn't important.

I really wanted to talk about something else and asked her, "So, what have you been up to so far this summer?"

"I've been doing some multiplication facts."

"Really? You've started learning to **multiply** already?"

"Yeah. My mommy says I need to get ready for the third grade since we'll be going back to school in a few weeks."

"Which ones have you learned already?" I asked, trying so hard to keep my mind off the boys.

"I learned that any number times 0 always equals 0."

"Teach me."

"You know, like 1 x 0 = 0. Even 50 x 0 = 0. Any number times 0 equals 0."

"Oh, so 10 x 0 = 0?"

"Yep."

"1,020 x 0 = 0?"

"Yep. You got it," Chanté said and clapped her hands.

"Cool. Any more?"

"Um, any number times 1 equals that number. Like 1 x 50 = 50. Or 50 x 1 = 50."

"So 12 x 1 = 12 and 11 x 1 = 11 and 10 x 1 = 10?"

"Yeah, but why are you doing them backwards? I go from 1 to 12 and not 12 down."

"I don't know." We both laughed. "Can I ask you something?"

"Sure. Go ahead."

"Do you like boys now?"

"No way!" she blurted out.

"Well, thank goodness you don't. It sure looks like Brooke does."

"Boys stink."

"I think so too," I told her.

I guess I did have a secret. Not just the fact that Trey said Brooke was pretty. I guess I wanted boys to think I was pretty too. And not because I wanted to like them back, but just because. Oh, well. All of this made me think about my cousin Sam. It's important to know how you feel about yourself deep down. But what could I do about it? Probably nothing. Oh, well.

● ● ● ● ●

"I can't believe it's been three weeks since we've been out here," Drake said, as we walked through the woods at the back of my house.

We were headed down our path to find the getaway

spot to our make-believe land. Drake was a little grumpy lately, and Sadie was acting strangely too. I wonder if they knew about Sam struggling with her weight and stuff. Maybe they were upset because they couldn't say anything.

If I asked them about it, I would have to tell what I knew too. Maybe that wasn't such a bad thing. Oh! I was sick and tired of being confused. It was just another couple weeks until my birthday. When I have another birthday, will I instantly become smarter? I hoped I wouldn't be so confused all the time.

"Where were we?" Drake said, as he kicked a pile of dirt.

"I don't know, and I don't have a good feeling about this. Maybe something happened to Bright," said Sadie.

"We gotta find her," Drake said, getting excited about the action and drama we were imagining.

"We can't tell the story that way. We told Bright we would keep her safe," I said, not wanting anything to happen to our make-believe friend.

"When it's your turn to tell the story, you can tell it anyway you want to. But my way and my sister's way is our way," Drake said, acting tough and getting all in my face.

"What's wrong with you?" I said, pushing him back a little.

"He's just mad," Sadie said. "Alec and his brother came home yesterday. And when they saw Drake, they called him a shrimp."

"Be quiet. You can't keep anything to yourself."

"Alec's back?" I asked. My voice sounded like I was happy about it.

"Yeah. Why are you sayin' it like you care?" Drake asked.

"Morgan likes Alec! Morgan likes Alec!" Sadie teased.

"I do not. It's just that we were becoming friends, and he's been gone all summer. But if he called you a shrimp, I don't think he's a person I wanna be friends with."

"Really?" Drake said. He sounded pleased that I wouldn't want anyone to tease him.

These kids were my cousins. And if anyone didn't wanna be their friend, they couldn't be my friend either. I thought Alec had changed. Maybe his brother put him up to calling Drake names. Either way, Drake was family. I would choose him before anyone else.

"We were right here," Drake said, feeling proud that he found our spot.

"We went too far again, y'all. And I don't wanna get in trouble this time," I said. I also didn't want to get lost.

"Morgan, we won't be out here too long. We'll find Bright, tell the story, and head back in."

Feeling like I didn't have a choice, I said," Okay. But, there's one thing we have to agree on."

"What's that?"

"You tell me what's wrong with you. Are you bummed out because those boys called you a shrimp?"

"Alec didn't call me a shrimp. It was his stupid brother,

Antoine. I'm two years older than Alec and he's taller than me. I just wish I was taller than him."

"My dad always told me that boys grow later than girls. And since Daddy Derek is your uncle, and he's tall, that means you're probably gonna get taller. It's in your blood."

"Yeah, I guess so. You're sittin' here tellin' all my secrets, Sadie," Drake said, as he tossed a pebble at his little sister. Sadie moved before it could hit her.

"Wait. What's he talkin' about?"

"Nothin'."

"She was in the bathroom staring at Sam."

"Oh, no. You mean, y'all know about Sam?"

"What do you mean, know about her? She's our sister. Sadie's jealous that Sam's hair is way longer than hers. Sam's hair goes all the way down her back."

"And mine doesn't. It just doesn't grow like that. Gosh! What's the big deal, Drake?" Sadie threw a twig at her brother. He caught it and stuck his tongue out at her.

"I like the way you wear your hair," I said. "That's a really cute style."

"You don't understand, Morgan. You have everything," Sadie said.

"My life is not perfect. How can you sit here and say that to me? I'm worried sick about my dad being in the Navy and fighting for our country. Every day, I feel sad because he's not here with me. I worry that he's not safe."

Sadie saw that I was getting sad, so she reached over and patted my back. "I'm sorry, Morgan, I didn't mean it like that. And even though you worry about your dad, at least you know your father. I mean, you're blessed to have two dads who care about you. You have a beautiful house to live in. What do you have to **complain** about?"

"When I went to a party yesterday, none of the boys thought I was pretty," I said, holding back tears. It made me realize how much this was bothering me. "They thought I was just a tomboy, who wanted to get dirty and play kickball."

"That stuff used to be fun for you," Drake said, remembering when I used to want to help with all of the hard chores.

"I think that's just it. A part of me doesn't want to do those things anymore."

All of a sudden, Sadie shouted, "Bright's gone, y'all! We need to stop havin' a pity party and find our friend."

"Okay, it's my turn to tell the story," Drake said. "So, the three of us set off to find Bright, the pink chipmunk who left her family because she didn't like how she looks. She got lost in the mean snake village called Dreadful Land, and we couldn't find her. Finally, after searching a long time, the three kids spotted a bright pink, furry object.

"Bright was being held in prison behind some super sharp porcupine needles. And those lime green, slimy snakes were zigzagging back and forth, watching guard over her."

"Oh, no! I can see her," I called.

"Where?" Sadie asked.

"Just look over there to the left!" And then I picked up where Drake left off.

"Bright spotted a line of blue ants. She told them to find the kids and warn her friends to watch out for the traps that the snakes had set up. Just when the three kids were about to come up with a plan to break Bright free, Mr. Oak Tree came alive. 'If you're not here by tomorrow to break her out, Bright will never be seen again.'"

"That's good, Morgan! We've got to come back tomorrow," Drake said. "We have to come up with a plan to free our friend."

We were having so much fun that we forgot about the things that were making us feel **insecure**.

As soon as we got back to the house, the three of us washed up quickly and sat down to eat.

"Where's Sam?" Sadie asked.

My mom said, "She's not feeling good. I really want her to eat, but she's not up to it. I'm going to have to take her to the doctor."

Oh, my goodness! Sam was feeling worse? Or maybe she was okay and just didn't feel like eating. At that moment, I felt so bad for keeping secrets.

Letter to Dad

Dear Dad,

Okay, Dad, so I've kept my cousin Sam's secret on purpose. I can't even tell you. I feel miserable for staying quiet though, because I think something is wrong. There is no monetary reward for being silent. I just want to help her. Of course she is thrilled because I didn't tell. Maybe I'll tell you later.

I've been learning some new things this summer, like how to multiply. I've learned a few multiplication facts. It's sort of fun. So when I learn the harder ones this year, I won't complain.

Dad, one more thing, I found out that lots of kids are insecure about something and it bothers them. I'm one of them. Pray for me. I don't feel pretty.

Your daughter,
Feeling ugly, Morgan

Word Search

```
J   M   U   L   T   I   I   P   T   I   O   N
S   E   P   T   H   E   N   B   E   R   J   E
E   L   B   A   R   E   S   I   M   D   C   T
T   H   L   M   I   A   E   T   O   G   O   A
Q   U   I   C   L   U   C   O   N   C   M   R
M   R   D   E   L   G   U   B   E   O   P   Y
A   L   N   V   E   U   R   E   T   M   L   E
Y   O   Z   R   D   S   E   R   A   P   A   S
M   A   R   C   H   T   F   X   R   L   I   P
B   M   U   L   T   I   P   L   Y   N   N   R
J   A   N   U   A   R   Y   J   U   N   E   U
A   P   R   I   L   E   S   O   P   R   U   P
```

COMPLAIN

INSECURE

MISERABLE

MONETARY

MULTIPLY

PURPOSE

THRILLED

Words to Know and Learn

1) **pur·pose** (pûr'pəs) *noun*
An intentional act

2) **mis·er·a·ble** (mĭz'ər-ə-bəl, mĭz'rə-) *adjective*
Very uncomfortable or unhappy

3) **mon·e·tar·y** (mŏn'ĭ-tĕr'ē, mŭn'-) *adjective*
Having to do with money

4) **thrill·ed** (thrĭl-d) *verb* (past tense)
To give great pleasure to; delight

5) **mul·ti·ply** (mŭl'tə-plī') *verb*
To add a positive number to itself a certain number of times; to do multiplication

6) **com·plain** (kəm-plān') *verb*
To express feelings of pain, dissatisfaction, or resentment

7) **in·se·cure** (ĭn'sĭ-kyʊr') *adjective*
Not sure or certain; doubtful

Chapter 6

Make Believe

Daddy Derek was so excited about the fun and exciting things going on at his church. Well, it was my church now too. I had never been to Vacation Bible School before. For five nights in a row, we've been having fun playing games, singing praises to God, and learning a great message. We even have snacks. So far it's been super fun. This is the last night, and I don't want it to end.

Drake, Sadie, and I are in the same class. We've been learning about Judges, chapter 6, and a man named Gideon. The theme for the week was: "You Have All You Need."

As soon as we got to class, our teacher, Deacon Ford, was ready with questions.

"All right, who can give me a summary so far of the story about Gideon?"

No one raised their hand.

"Come on, guys. Let's talk and explore. We've been having such a good time this week. Now it's time to bring the message home. No one wants to share?"

Everyone, including me, just stared at Deacon Ford. So he made his face look real sad, but we all knew he was kidding. It was one of his tricks to make us laugh as we learned the lesson.

When we started to feel bad for him, one by one all of our hands shot straight up into the air. Deacon Ford called on Drake first.

"Go ahead, young man."

"In the story of Gideon, we know that the children of Israel had been doin' a lot of bad stuff. Then God allowed their enemies, the Midianites, to defeat them for seven years. I mean, they tore up the town and stole their flocks of sheep. They took everything that the Israelites had. So the children of Israel got scared and went into the mountains and hid in caves."

Sadie raised her hand high and said, "He's talked enough. My turn!"

"Okay, young lady," Deacon Ford said. "Take the story from here."

"Well, while they were hiding, God sent a prophet to let them know He was going to deliver them from the bad people and stuff so they didn't need to be afraid. He wanted them to get the message and obey Him. Then they'd be able to conquer the Midianites. But they still wouldn't listen. So one day, an angel came to this guy named Gideon. He was afraid and hiding too. The angel said, *'The Lord is with you, mighty warrior.'* But Gideon had low self-**esteem,** which means he didn't think very highly about himself. So he didn't think he was any kind of a brave soldier."

Sadie was feeling pretty good about her answer, and Deacon Ford let her go on.

"And that's the first lesson we learned. It's not about what you think you have. God wasn't looking at Gideon the way that Gideon looked at himself. Gideon was very afraid, but God could make him strong. He just had to believe that God had the power. That's what we've gotta do too. We've gotta trust and believe in God because He sees us for what we can be."

"Wow, that's very good, Miss Sadie. Anyone else?" Deacon Ford asked.

I raised my hand. "God helped Gideon a lot. He knew Gideon needed proof that God had sent the angel. Then, the Bible says, *'The Spirit of the Lord came on Gideon, and he blew a trumpet.'* That means when the Lord is with us, we can do mighty things. So Gideon trusted God, and he was ready to lead an **uprising** against the Midianites. But God didn't want the army to be too big because He wanted the people to know that only His strength could defeat their enemies. So He told Gideon to make most of the men go back home. God only wanted a few men to fight."

"Very good, Miss Love. And that's where we are right now. Once you believe that God is with you, you can feel

His power and do great things. Here's another example. The Spirit of the Lord got a hold of Dr. Martin Luther King Jr., and he led the Black people in America to **demand** their rights as a people. I'm sure he was probably scared sometimes. But when he felt God's covering and believed His promise, Dr. King stepped up. Because of that, you guys can go to school wherever you want, and you can become whatever you want to be in life. And, know that sometimes when you step up, it's not about you. It's about the purpose God has given you to help others. Do you understand?"

"Yes, sir," we all said together.

"Good. Now, to wrap this up," Deacon Ford said, "Remember this. When it was time for battle, God did most of the fighting. Gideon and his men had their lamps and trumpets. And when Gideon gave the signal, they all blew their horns at the same time. Then they opened up those lamps and held up the torches. Because they obeyed God, Gideon's army of 300 men defeated over 2,000 Midianites. And God wanted it this way so that no one could brag on what they did on their own. Clearly, it was the Lord who helped them win the battle."

This was a great story, and we were all listening really hard. Then Deacon Ford told us some more important news.

"We need to remember that Jesus is always with us. We need to give Him the credit for the good things that happen in our lives. And we must trust Him when things are not going so good too. If you trust Him, He will make everything right. Remember, it's not what you think you are, but who Jesus knows you are. That makes you somebody special, and you can have good self-esteem because of Jesus. Life is like a long race. Because you are a child of the King, nothing can stop you from winning in the end. Even if you don't like how you look, how much money you have, or anything else you think you're missing, just believe that the Lord loves you. Don't ever stop trusting Him because He didn't make any mistakes. Always remember that God made you worth more than all the gold and everything else of value on this earth."

I looked over at Drake and at Sadie and we smiled at each other. The three of us were having trouble with different things but hearing the story of Gideon gave us the courage we needed. It wasn't what we thought of ourselves, but what God thinks about us that makes us strong. And we felt good about knowing that.

Then it was time for cake and ice cream! And that made the day really cool. We'd had a great lesson, and now it was time to have more fun. Yes!

• • • • •

"We gotta finish the story," Drake said, as Sadie and I followed him down the path a week later.

"I know we have to find Bright, but it's Saturday, and I wanted to sleep in. I'll be going back to school in another week," I said, moaning.

"Well, you're up now," Drake said. "Our mom will be here in a few days to take us home for good and then we won't be able to finish the story."

"Yeah, you're right," I said, not happy about that. I knew I was really gonna miss them.

"Look! Here's the last place we were lookin' for Bright," Sadie said. She was ready to get the story moving. "I'll go first."

While Drake and I searched for a spot to sit, Sadie just wanted us to hurry up. After Drake cleared some twigs away, we sat on the ground and Sadie told her story.

"The kids were lookin' for Bright, and they came to a huge rock. The rock was eight feet tall and five feet wide. It looked like it had been there for a lot of years. All of a sudden, the big rock started to roll away, and three giant pit bulls surrounded the three kids."

"I'll take over," I said, trying to wonder where in the world her story was going. "The three pit bulls wouldn't stop barking until one of the kids said, 'Wait! We're lookin' for our friend, Bright. She's a pink chipmunk who was taken away from us by the snake family. Have you seen her?' Then the dogs stopped barking, and the biggest pit bull said, 'All you had to do was ask.'"

"Wait. You're gonna make the pit bulls nice and helpful to the kids? What kinda scary story is that?" asked Drake.

"Can you be quiet, please?" I said, giving him a mean stare.

"This is my story. Now, where was I? Oh yeah. The

kids followed the pit bulls down a **winding** path, and every one of the scary animals stayed away from them. All of the forest creatures knew the pit bulls had special powers. The dogs had an invisible shield around them so the bears couldn't get them. The lions couldn't get them. And the slimy snakes couldn't get them either.

"Then it started to rain, and the invisible shield couldn't protect the kids anymore. The lightning and thunder sounded so loud that the kids got scared and the pit bulls disappeared. The kids spotted a cave, and they ran inside to protect themselves from all the animals they had seen when they were under the invisible shield."

Sadie interrupted me. "This reminds me of the story of Gideon. In our mind, we're in a cold, dark cave too . . . so cool."

"Yeah, a make-believe one," said Drake. "But you gotta remember, just like in the story of Gideon, our enemies out there are tryin' to rip us apart. We just gotta know that we can beat 'em."

"Yeah. But we have to know that it's not just our power and strength alone," I reminded them. "We have to use the power of the Lord."

"Okay, let's pray," Drake said.

We bowed our heads, and I said, "Lord, we learned a good lesson in Vacation Bible School this summer about self-esteem and knowing who we are in Your eyes. We're making up this story about trying to find a pink chipmunk, and right now we're afraid to fight the scary animals. We need You to help us. That's the reason why we've been tellin' this creepy, make-believe story. We've been trying to keep it a secret, but our self-esteem is low. Drake wants to be taller. Sadie wants longer hair. I don't think I'm pretty enough. And Sam, well, You know, Lord. We just need Your help. Help us see what You see, and help us to know that we're good enough just the way that we are. In Jesus' name. Amen."

"What about Sam?" Sadie couldn't wait to ask.

"Who cares about her? She's probably at the house taking a nap or something. Didn't you get the message? We already have the power," Drake said.

Then he stood up to finish the story. "Then all of the kids put their hands together and said '1–2–3 dynamite!' So let's do it, y'all."

So we all grabbed hands and screamed, "1–2–3 dynamite!"

After that, Drake continued, "Then the brave three rushed out of the cave. And the next thing they knew, they were in the Land of the Snakes. It was quiet and all the snakes were sleepin'. The kids were able to **slither** past the snake guards better than a snake could. Once they passed the gates, they screamed out. They made so much noise that all the snakes woke up and got tangled up in each other tryin' to defend themselves. In the middle of the craziness, the kids saw Bright. They were able to rescue her and get her out of that bad place."

Sadie picked up from there. "Then Bright asked, 'What

took y'all so long?' So the three kids hugged Bright real tight."

"We're so glad to see you, Bright!" I added.

"I just wanna go back home. I'm sorry for runnin' away just because I don't like the way I look. I know my family misses me. Can you guys help me get home?"

"We can't help her get home right now," Drake said, as he looked at his watch. "Uncle Derek wants us to come back. He's gonna take us someplace."

"Bright, we're gonna give you a new hidin' place. We need you to stay here until we come back and then we'll get you home," Sadie said.

The spot we picked to put Bright in was high up in the tree. I couldn't reach it and Sadie couldn't either. So Drake reached as high as he could. He stretched and stretched some more to get to the spot. Then he knew that he could do something that a taller person could do. He acted like he put Bright way up high. We told her bye and started home.

• • • • •

Mom had curled Sadie's hair the night before. Sadie cried out because the rollers were so tight. Although Sadie didn't have long hair, it looked very pretty in curls. But after playing in the woods, her curls had fallen.

On the way back to the house, Sadie said, "I really do like my hair. Drake is okay with his height. Do you like yourself, Morgan?"

I shrugged my shoulders. "I guess."

When she said that, I was so glad that they felt good about themselves that I didn't care about me at the moment. I really liked my cousins, and it was cool that they were happier. Guess I was growing up or something.

As soon as we got home, Daddy Derek told us to quickly wash up and get ready for our trip. Pretty soon we all piled into the car.

"We're gonna have a great time. I wish we'd made Sam come too," Mom said to Daddy Derek, as we pulled into the parking lot of the Dr. Martin Luther King, Jr. Center.

Mom got me all excited about what we were about to do. Drake, Sadie, and I had just learned something about Dr. Martin Luther King, Jr. in Vacation Bible School. He was a great man, and, after all, we have a day off school in January as we honor his birthday. Although we don't live very far from this special place, I'd never been here, and I really wanted to find out more about Dr. King.

First, we saw the **memorial** graves of Dr. King and his wife, Coretta Scott King. Drake was the first one to say, "Wow!"

It was a beautiful place. As we went through the museum, we learned they were both great people who weren't afraid to help African Americans have a better place in America and in the world too.

Dr. King had a dream. He believed that all people are created equal, no matter the color of their skin. He believed being Black was something good because God made us. He also thought that no one should let somebody else keep them from becoming all they could be. Each person must learn to have self-esteem and to stand up for themselves.

The sad part about it was that he died while he was still fighting for what he believed in and didn't even get to see his four children grow up. Sometimes, when God wants us to stand for something big, we might have to pay a big price for doing it. But, God will give that person a big reward too.

I was glad to be learning all this good stuff, but I just kept thinking about Sam. She was so sad. She hadn't been eating much. And the little she did eat, she didn't keep down. And it was wrong for me to keep all of this a secret from my mom.

When it was time to leave, I wanted to go straight home. But my family wanted to go to a restaurant called the Varsity. It's a place in downtown Atlanta that serves some of the best hot dogs and French fries. But I didn't wanna go there. I wanted to go and check on Sam.

When he heard me whisper to Mom that we should go home now, Drake said. "She's all right." He was rubbing his stomach and acting like he was starving or something.

He didn't know everything about his sister. I knew that she wasn't okay.

Mom agreed with me. "I just don't feel comfortable. We should get back home right away. Plus, the baby's been fussy. We can get something to eat later."

"I'll put some hot dogs on the grill," Daddy Derek said.

"Uncle Derek, I'm not tryin' to talk about your cooking

or anything, but your hot dogs don't even come close to the delicious ones at the Varsity. I remember when you took me there before. It was soooo good. Come on, please."

"Let's get back home to check on your sister," Daddy Derek replied.

"But we just left Dr. Martin Luther King Jr. Center."

We all looked at Drake, wondering what he was talking about.

"What does that have to do with anything?" asked Daddy Derek.

"Well, I had a dream I was eating a Varsity hot dog."

"Boy, you're so silly." Sadie hit him lightly, and I poked him playfully too.

When we got home, Mom called out to Sam but she didn't answer. She was downstairs watching TV when we left, so Drake and Sadie headed down there to look for her in the family room.

"She's not down here!" Sadie called out to us.

"Maybe she's upstairs sleeping," Mom said. "I'll go check on her."

When my parents looked in the guest room, I went straight to the bathroom. The light was on, and the door was slightly open.

"Sam? Are you in there? I called out.

She had to be in there. When she didn't answer right away, my heart started beating faster, and I felt yucky.

Something wasn't right. I listened closely and heard

water running. When I pushed the door open wider, there was Sam bending over the bathroom sink. She just looked up at me with a weird look.

"Morgan, call your Mom. I'm sick. I need to go to the doctor now," Sam said weakly.

"Mom!" I screamed.

I heard Daddy Derek's footsteps.

"She's in here," I said.

He came just in time to catch Sam before she fell to the floor.

When Mom reached the bathroom door, she saw the scene and the look on Sam's face. She rushed to her side.

"Sam! What's wrong?" Mom asked in a **panic.**

Sam didn't answer her.

"You get her ready, and I'll call her mom. We've got to get her to the hospital right away!" Daddy Derek said.

Drake, Sadie, and I stood back out of the way. We were all in shock.

As he rushed out to start the car, we must have looked pretty scared. "She'll be all right, guys. Morgan, you need to wait here with your cousins," Daddy Derek told us.

"There's no time to waste," Mom said to him. "You go on ahead, and I'll follow. I have to call my mother to come over so she can stay with the baby and the kids."

We watched as Daddy Derek picked up Sam in his arms and carried her to the car.

Drake was the one who didn't even wanna come home and check on his sister. I knew all kinds of bad things were going through his mind. I could tell by the look on his face how worried he was.

"She's gonna be okay," I told him.

"Don't worry, Drake. Sam is tough," Sadie said as she grabbed her brother's arm.

My mom was so worried. I was too, but it helped when Mama showed up to sit with us.

"Mommy, is Sam gonna be all right?"

"We have to pray and trust God, sweetheart. I should have known something was wrong. I felt it when she kept acting so strange about eating. I've been concerned about her. I tried to talk to her. I even asked her mom if I could make a doctor's appointment for her on Monday. And here we find her almost passed out. Oh, my goodness. I'm so glad we came home when we did."

I was gonna have to tell her what I knew. But for now I just closed my eyes and pretended Sam was okay. This just wasn't happening. It was like a bad dream. Somehow, this all had to be make believe.

Letter to Dad

Dear Dad,

Something is always going on with me. There has been an **uprising** here. Let me explain. We went on a trip and my cousin Sam didn't want to go. I should have **demanded** that she go or I'd tell what I knew. But, she stayed home.

All the time we were at the Dr. Martin Luther King Jr. Center, I was thinking about her. On the **winding** tour, you have to be quiet, so I had to **slither** over to Mom. I quietly told her I thought we should go check on Sam. Once we'd seen the great **memorial**, we did go home.

Dad, we were all in a **panic** when we found Sam sick and almost passed out. She needs help. Sam has to work on her **self-esteem** because, as pretty as she is, she thinks she's not good enough. This has been so scary.

> Your daughter,
> Very worried, Morgan

Word Search

```
S  D  R  A  W  U  P  O  N  N  O  W
T  E  S  T  E  E  M  H  I  M  G  I
E  M  F  R  I  E  N  D  S  N  N  N
P  A  E  B  E  S  T  J  I  S  I  D
H  N  M  M  P  C  A  S  R  L  D  U
A  D  O  Z  O  O  I  C  E  I  N  P
N  P  O  B  P  R  D  U  H  T  I  L
I  E  R  U  P  B  I  A  I  H  W  N
W  R  I  U  E  W  E  A  L  E  U  D
J  Y  P  A  N  I  C  D  L  R  Z  O
F  P  I  C  N  I  C  A  L  E  C  N
A  U  T  H  O  R  S  M  O  O  R  E
```

DEMAND

ESTEEM

MEMORIAL

PANIC

SLITHER

UPRISING

WINDING

Words to Know and Learn

1) up·ris·ing (ŭp'rī'zĭng) *noun*
A rebellion

2) de·mand (dĭ–mănd') *verb*
To ask to be informed of something

3) wind·ing (wīn'dĭng) *adjective*
A curve or bend, as on a tour path or a road

4) es·teem (ĭ–stēm') *noun*
High opinion, respect

5) slith·er (slĭTH'ər) *verb*
To walk with a sliding or shuffling gait

6) me·mo·ri·al (mə–môr'ē–əl, –mōr'–) *noun*
Something, such as a monument or holiday, intended to celebrate or honor the memory of a person or an event

7) pan·ic (păn'ĭk) *noun*
A sudden, overpowering terror, often affecting many people at once

Chapter 7

So Sweet

As I stood there in the doorway watching Mommy drive off, I prayed, *Lord, please let Sam make it through this okay. I feel so horrible that this is all my fault. I shouldn't have kept the secret for her. Even though she didn't want me to tell about why she wasn't eating, I knew I should have said something. Lord, please help.*

I went into the kitchen to find Mama. I could always count on her to help me when I was in trouble. Mama was getting a bottle of milk for Jayden from the refrigerator.

Before I even said a word, she asked, "What's wrong, sweetie?"

I looked over at the countertop and there was a piece of chocolate cake. It had been barely touched. Mama saw what I was looking at. She had noticed the cake too.

My tears started falling. I already knew why the cake

was left there, and now it was time for me to let everyone else know.

"Morgan," she came over to me and asked, "do you know something about this? Talk to me, please."

"Yes, I do. It's all my fault!"

"How is this your fault, Morgan? What do you mean?" she asked.

"Mama, I knew she was sick. I knew what she was doing with her food, but I didn't know how to tell anyone. Sam made me promise not to say anything, so I didn't. I'm so sorry."

"Oh, my goodness. Morgan, hasn't your mom always told you that you can't keep some things a secret? Even so, honey, this isn't your fault. You didn't make Sam do this to herself. But, whenever you feel that something is wrong with you or anybody else, it's always best to tell your mom or me what's on your heart. We care about you and the things that bother you. That way we'll be able to help you work things out."

• • • • •

Mom and Daddy Derek told us later what happened at the hospital.

After Daddy Derek signed some papers, he and Mom waited in the **emergency** room for the doctor to talk to them.

"Samantha is resting now. She was quite a sick young lady. How long has it been since she stopped eating properly?" the doctor asked.

"She's been staying with us over the summer months. Sam is my sister's child. We've phoned her and she's on her way," said Daddy Derek.

Then Mom spoke. "She's been careful to obey us whenever we tell her to finish her meal. We just didn't know that she would make herself throw up later on. I feel terrible. I should have known something was wrong with her. I just had no idea she would do something as serious as this."

"My sister told me that Sam has been acting kind of strange for some time. She's a single mom and works long hours. She feels bad that she hadn't taken Sam to the doctor before now. She didn't realize how serious it was either."

"Well, you can go in and see her now. I want to talk with you all and Sam after you spend some time with her. I'll join you a little later," said the doctor.

He showed Mom and Daddy Derek the room Sam was in and walked away. Sam was sitting up in bed looking very sad and afraid. As soon as she saw my parents, she started to cry.

"Don't cry, Sam," Mom said to her. "I'm so sorry that I didn't know what you were going through. I wish you had talked to me about how you were feeling."

"I knew you wouldn't understand. I had to do it. I need to look like my friends at school. But they have better clothes to wear, and they're all much smaller than me."

"Honey, don't you know how pretty you are? You don't

need cool clothes to feel good about yourself. You just have to know that you're a special person just the way that you are." said Daddy Derek.

"No one tells me that. So how could I know? None of the boys at school seem to like me the way they do the other girls."

"Sam, that will come soon enough," Mom said. "Right now, you should focus on studying and keeping yourself healthy. I had to do it when I was your age. And one of the best ways to take care of yourself is to eat properly. I'm sorry there's been so much **pressure** on you to fit in. But you first have to feel good about yourself on the inside. You'll be surprised at how others will notice a **positive** difference in you."

There was a knock on the door, and the doctor entered the room.

"Well, young lady, how are you feeling now?"

"I feel better, thank you."

"Doctor, what causes this kind of problem in children? And what can parents do about it?" Mom asked.

The doctor then explained to Mom, Daddy Derek, and Sam that a lot of young girls are having trouble like this.

"Eating disorders can begin very early in a child's life. Many times it starts because a girl is unhappy with her body shape. This can be caused by many reasons. But a big part of the problem today is that children get the idea from TV, movies, books, and magazines that being thin is the most important way to be.

"Sometimes this message starts to affect a girl's self-esteem. She begins to look around her and sees her body shape differently than everyone else sees her. Often problems with self-esteem begin when someone is making fun of a girl and she begins to feel bad because she may be bigger than her friends and other classmates.

"Most of the time when a girl is sad and unhappy with the way she looks, the first thing she will try to do is change on her own. If she thinks that she looks too big, she will eat as little as possible or stop eating anything at all. Some girls don't eat breakfast and lunch at school, and their parents don't even know it. Then at dinnertime, a girl might eat but will make herself throw up the food after dinner, just to keep from gaining weight.

"When a girl doesn't eat properly, she might faint sometimes, and her heart can beat in an uneven way. And this can have a big effect on the normal way in which a girl grows up.

"Many parents don't know their child is having a problem like this until they have to bring her to the hospital. So parents must pay attention to the signs. If the child seems afraid of gaining weight, if all of a sudden she's making poor grades in school, if she seems to worry all the time, or if she acts out when she can't get her way, this kind of behavior often goes along with her poor eating habits. Other changes to watch for in the way a girl behaves are if a girl begins to complain all the time and has more trouble handling problems than before.

"That's why it's so important for parents to help their children form a positive image of themselves. The best thing a parent can do to help is to spend time gently talking to the child, encourage healthy eating at home by providing healthy meals, and take the child to the doctor for regular check-ups. If the child is already showing signs of having an eating disorder, the parent can find a support group for her to attend. Many times talking about their problems with other kids their age can help a lot."

The doctor finished by saying, "But, for now we have to help Samantha get well. So, we're going to keep her for a few days to build her back up. Is that okay with you, young lady?"

Sam just nodded her head sadly. But in her heart she was ready for a positive change.

● ● ● ● ●

After Daddy Derek and Mom came back home, they told us Sam was going to be all right. Everyone in the house was relieved. Even Jayden seemed happier.

I was sitting on my bed reading a book when Mom knocked on the door. I could tell from the look on her face that she had something serious to say. It was a look that let me know how unhappy she was with me. It was like I'd gotten all Fs on my report card.

Mom started to drill me. "Morgan, your grandmother told me that you knew about Sam. I know you're at the age when you want people to like you. And I know you're getting along better with your cousins, but sweetheart, we've had this talk before. There are some things you simply cannot keep from me."

"I know, Mom, I just didn't think. I am so sorry. I'm so glad that's she's going to be okay."

"She is. But because her body is so weak, it's going to take some time.

"Is that what the doctor said?"

"Yes. It's important for her to get enough fluid and food back into her system so that she will be healthy again. Now, I can't really blame you for not speaking up because she was under my care. I should have watched her more and questioned why she didn't want to eat. Both of us need grace," Mom said, hugging me.

As she smiled at me, she was wiping tears from her eyes.

Then I heard Daddy Derek calling us kids to the dining room table. Each one had a piece of Mama's chocolate cake and a glass of milk in front of us.

"Have a seat, kids, and enjoy this little treat. I know that your grandmother made sure you all ate your dinner."

At first the four of us were eating quietly, but all of a sudden, it was broken by his words.

Daddy Derek said, "You know what, guys? We need to talk about this whole self-esteem thing because you all are growing up, and sometimes you're not happy with yourselves. Yeah, I know everyone talked about self-esteem at Vacation Bible School, but I need to make sure that you all understand that you're fine just the way God made you. Sure, there are things you can work on, like studying hard to be the best student you can be, but you have to be wise about what you can and cannot change."

"Oh, my goodness," Sadie said, as she broke down and cried. Even though she knew her sister was going to be okay, she just started bawling.

Drake looked at me with a mean stare. "I can't believe you didn't say anything."

"Don't be mad at her," Sadie said to him. "Sam told us before we came over here that she didn't like her body. We knew she wasn't eating right. We're just as much to blame as anybody. She's our sister!"

Daddy Derek said, "Nobody needs to take the blame. We all have to be thankful that the Lord was with her. And He's with us all. What I'm saying to you three is that I care about you. And you don't have to carry your problems all by yourself. If there's something that you need to say, let's talk about it. We could have kept things from getting this serious for Sam had we known sooner."

"Well, Drake wishes he was taller," Sadie blurted out.

"Uncle Derek, I was struggling with that before, but I'm over it now. I grew up this summer. Can't you tell?"

"I see a positive change in you, son. You know, I was short in elementary school. But in middle school I sprouted up. I have some friends who aren't very tall, but that isn't stopping them from doing amazing things. It's okay to want to improve something, but it's not okay to be so down on yourself that you're not thankful for what God has already given you."

Drake blabbed, "Well, Sadie's talkin' about me, but she wishes her hair was longer. Ha! I told on you too."

"I like my style now. I know that my hair isn't gonna grow longer like some girls hair grows. But, I don't care what anybody says, my hair is cool with me," Sadie said, working her fingers through what was left of her curls.

"Yeah, right. You know you wish it was longer," Drake teased, as they both smiled. "But, for real, sis, your hair looks all right."

"Now, Morgan. Sadie seems to be okay with the way she looks and Drake is more comfortable with his height. What about you?" Daddy Derek asked.

I had to think. What about me? Did I like the way I looked?

"I should have known better than to keep Sam's secret. I try too hard to please people. I want to be strong and smart like my mom. I wish I was pretty like her too."

"You are pretty," he said, placing his hand gently on my shoulder. "You are a cute girl on the outside. And even better, you have a big heart, and that makes you something special on the inside."

"You really think so?"

"I really know so," he said to me, as he leaned over and gave me a big hug.

After we finished eating, he prayed, "Lord, I thank You for these young people who have a heart to know You more. Let them know that You created them in the image of You. Let them know they're great just the way You made them. We also thank You for taking care of Sam. We don't deserve Your goodness and mercy, but we are so grateful to You. In Jesus' name we pray. Amen."

All three of us together said, "Amen."

• • • • •

"Longitude goes up and down. Latitude goes round and round. Longitude goes up and down. Latitude goes round and round. Come on, Morgan. Sing it with me," my cousin Sadie said. She, Drake, and I were walking through the woods to help Bright, our imaginary friend, find her way back home.

Confused by why she was dancing and what she was singing about, I asked, "What does that mean?"

"I'm doin' a cheer that helps me remember some **concepts** I learned in my geography lesson."

"Oh, so latitude and longitude are a part of geography?" I was trying to understand, as she nodded. "Well, why are you talkin' about latitude and longitude right now?"

She pointed at her brother. Drake was holding something small and round. It almost looked like a little clock. "Look at what Drake has. It's a compass."

"A compass? What's that?" I asked.

Drake showed me the clock-like thing he held in his hand. It had a circle face with a black arrow that pointed to different letters.

Then he told me, "It shows what direction you're going in. See the N at the top? It means north. The S at the bottom means south. On the right, there's an E for—? I know you know this, Morgan."

"East!" I said. Now I was getting what they were talking about.

He looked happy and said, "That's right! And what's on the left?"

Proudly, I shouted, "The W means west."

"Okay, exactly. And if the arrow is in between the N and E, that means northeast. If it's in between the N and the W, that's northwest. If it's between the S and the W, that's southwest, and if it's between the S and the E, that's southeast. I won my compass at school for having the highest social studies average in my grade. I figured since we were leaving today, we could use it to find out exactly what direction our imaginary place is from your house."

"Not only will we know if we're northeast, south, or whatever, but we can also know our latitude and longitude points," Sadie said, feeling proud of what she knew.

"Now, what's that?" I asked.

She explained, "Latitude is halfway between the north pole and the south pole, and it has an imaginary line."

"Really?" I said.

"Yeah, that line is called the **equator**."

"Oh, yeah I heard of the equator before."

"The equator goes around the middle of the earth. It's kinda like that cool silver belt you're wearin' around your waist. Girl, you need to let me take that home with me," Sadie said, touching the smooth material.

"Thanks. My birthday is comin' up soon. I'm thinkin' about wearin' it then."

"You should. It's cute."

"Am I gonna be invited to the party?" Drake asked. "Or is it just for girls?"

"I hope you come because I'm really gonna miss you guys," I said, letting them both know how I felt about them.

Sadie hugged me. "We're gonna miss you too."

"Hey, we were teachin' her somethin' here. Let's not get all **sentimental** and mushy," Drake said.

Sadie continued, "Okay, latitude starts at the equator and its 0. Above it is 10 degrees north and below it is 10 degrees south. It goes all the way to a total of 360 degrees. But longitude goes the other way, east and west. Longitude has a **prime meridian** in the middle."

"That sounds kinda confusing," I said.

"Yeah, but you're gonna learn about it next year. You'll be okay if you just remember that longitude goes up and down. And latitude goes round and round! Just keep singin' my song, and you'll be ready for it."

"And when you see a compass, you'll know what it is," said Drake. Then he stopped walking and said, "And, here we are. My compass is sayin' our spot is exactly NE, that's northeast from your house."

"And one day I'm gonna find the exact longitude and latitude points on the map!"

"Cool. Look, there's Bright! She's all safe and secure," Drake said, as he started our make-believe story.

"I'm ready to go home. I really miss my family," Sadie said, playing like Bright was talking. But my cousin's eyes had real tears in them.

"Sadie, why are you crying?" I asked.

"I'm sad because I really had fun with you this summer, Morgan. I never had a little sister before and bein' able to teach you stuff is cool. And now that my big sister is gonna be okay, I'm just feelin' happy and sad at the same time. That's all." She hugged me again.

"All right, all right. Cut the mushy, girly stuff out. Don't y'all see Bright jumpin' up and down? She's ready to go home."

"It's my turn," I said. "So the three kids led Bright back to Dream Land. The closer Bright and her friends got to her home, the more lots of chipmunks started cheering, 'She's back! She's back! She's back!'"

"The next thing they knew, a taller, older chipmunk came along," Drake added, "with his wife on his arm. The two chipmunks walked up to the three children and the daddy chipmunk said, 'You brought back our baby girl. Thank you! We thought she was gone forever.' And then Bright fell into her parents' arms."

"And, as they rubbed her soft pink fur," Sadie added. "Her mom said, 'I'm sorry I didn't make you feel special, because we love you dearly.' Then Bright spoke and said, 'I love you too, Mommy and Daddy. I ran away because I was bein' teased and I didn't think I was good enough. But now that I've been away, I learned that I am a special chipmunk because God made me just the way I am—a bright, neon pink color."

"Well, we'd better get goin'," Drake said to Bright. "We'll see you later to check in with you from time to time."

Before the three kids could leave, I took over the story and said, "Bright walked over to the kids and told them, 'You guys have gotten very close this summer while you were tryin' to help me get home. I wasn't happy with myself, and I knew the three of you weren't happy with yourselves either. But you've gotta know that you'll keep gettin' better and better. Drake, you are growing taller. Sadie, your hair looks great with the length you already have. You're still young and your hair will keep growing. And Morgan—"

I couldn't finish because I was the one telling the story. Drake quickly jumped in. "Then Bright said, 'And, Morgan, you're a very cute girl.' Can we leave now?"

That was very nice of him to say. We walked back to my house, knowing that our summer was pretty much over. We had done a good thing by helping our friend get back home. Besides, we helped each other feel better about ourselves. Now we have good self-esteem. We'd never forget this special place that is northeast of my house.

● ● ● ● ●

"It's my birthday!" I woke up and shouted the top of my voice.

Although I'd be going back to school in a few days, today was my day, and I couldn't wait for all of my friends to come over and have fun with me. It already seemed like a long time ago when we saw each other at Brooke's party. So I was ready for us to have a blast!

I rushed into Mom's room and said, "Why is my party in the afternoon? Can't it be earlier?"

"Happy Birthday, sweetie!" Mom said, hugging me.

Leading the way toward the kitchen, she said, "First, we have some things to do. We need enough time to get ready for your friends. So you can help me clean up, honey."

"But, it's my birthday. I shouldn't have to clean up," I said to her with an unhappy face.

With her hand on one hip, she handed me the dish towel and said, "Well, if you want to have friends over then you have to help get ready for them. If you hadn't helped to make a mess, then we wouldn't have anything to clean up. So let's not try to be too grown up. Okay?"

"Yes, ma'am, I just can't wait for the party, Mom. That's all!"

"I know, sweetie. And it's going to be fun."

Sure enough, after we finished all the chores, we decorated the backyard with pink and purple balloons. Then we set up the yard with different games for us kids to play. Mama and Papa showed up with the cake, and Daddy

Derek fired up the grill. If my friends didn't come soon, I was gonna pop worse than a balloon that got stuck with a needle. I was so excited and ready for my guests to arrive.

"A Field Day theme. What a great idea," Daddy Derek said to me, as the smell of yummy hot dogs, hamburgers, and chicken was starting to fill the air.

Mom thought of the idea since I didn't have the best memories of the Field Day event at the end of the school year. It was because I got into trouble for making fun of another student. With my birthday party having the same theme, it will give me a fun time to remember. Mom said now I'll be able to look forward to Field Day for years to come.

My cousins were the first to come. Sam gave me a big hug and handed me a gift. "Happy Birthday! This is from all of us," she said with a big smile.

"Thanks!" I reached out and took the pretty box from her.

"Can I talk to you for a second?"

"Yeah," I said, not sure of what she wanted to say.

When we were alone, Sam said, "Morgan, you were right. I shouldn't have been hurting myself the way that I was. And I was wrong to ask you not to tell anybody. I'm glad it's over. My mom took me to see another doctor and now I'm getting the help I need."

"Are you doin' better? Are you feelin' better? Do you like yourself now?" I asked, hoping the answers would be yes, yes, and yes.

And when they were, we hugged so tight. I never thought Sam and me would be cool because she was much older. She'd never been interested in me at all. Now, we could be closer as cousins who really share something special.

"Enough with all the huggin'," Drake said when he found us.

Then he asked me, "Can I be the captain of the blue team?"

"Sure. Here are some blue wristbands to pass out to your team when everybody gets here. My friends should be here soon."

"I wanna be a captain too," Sadie said. "You need four teams, right?"

"Yep, you can have the yellow team." I handed her the yellow bands.

"I won't be over a team, but I'm gonna be out there too. I'll be a judge watchin' over everything. The other two captains are gonna be Trey and Brooke. So with two girls and two boys, it's all even," I said.

Soon everyone was at the party. Altogether, I counted twenty friends and cousins, not including Sam and me. I divided the teams into four groups of five players.

Sadie was always ready to teach me something. She came up to me and said, "You know, Morgan, in the third grade you're gonna learn your times tables. Then you'll find out that 20 divided by 5 is 4."

"Okay," I said.

It was all right for her to want to help me get ready for the third grade, but right now all I cared about was the fun that my friends and I were getting ready to have.

Alec and his brother Antoine were there. Billy was there. So was Chanté. And, of course, my two best friends, Brooke and Trey. Billy was on Brooke's team, and they won the three-legged race. Trey had Antoine on his team, and they won the 100-yard dash. Alec was on Sadie's team, and they won the balloon toss. Drake had Chanté on his team and they won the bean toss. Every team won a prize. It was so fun!

When Daddy Derek said it was time to eat, we all rushed to the picnic tables.

"Oh, no. First, you all have to line up by the water hose. Use the soap over there and wash those hands. And don't forget to dry them with the paper towels," Mom told us.

Walking to the wash-up area, I saw Trey smiling at Brooke. He was looking at her like he did at her birthday party. Yes, she was as cute as ever, with her long curls and a colorful sundress. Brooke was smiling at him too.

"Do you like Trey?" I asked her.

"We're just friends. Besides, I'm not ready for boys."

"Brooke, you are very cool and really pretty too."

"Glad you think so because my best friend is really pretty too," she said, repeating what I told her and giving me a thumbs-up.

"You think I'm pretty?"

"Yeah!" She said, taking my hand and twirling me around. "My hair is so long and most of the time it gets on my nerves. To me, yours is just the right length. You always have a fresh style, Morgan, like you just walked out of the beauty shop or something. And you're good at sports too. Check out your birthday party. You get to hang with the boys and wear the coolest sports clothes. Work it, Morgan. You are so cool."

"She is cool and pretty too, huh?" Alec whizzed by the two of us and said. He seemed to be in a big hurry as he hurried past us on his way to get a burger and some punch. Both of us just laughed at him.

But then my laughing quickly turned into almost tears. I took my friend's hand and said, "I was so jealous of you, Brooke, thinking I was ugly."

She just smiled, and her eyes got wide. "So you're not perfect after all. I was so mad at you last year, and I was wrong for that. But I'm glad to know that you make mistakes too. You don't have to be jealous of me, Morgan. You've got it goin' on better than me. We're buddies, and we should keep it that way. Now, can we go and eat? And, aren't you ready for some cake?"

I was so happy we had that talk, I said, "Yeah! I'm ready for it all!"

Arm-in-arm, we skipped over to the table and sat next to each other. She had no idea how she had made my day. I felt so blessed.

Looking around at my family and friends, I had learned

some great lessons. When we first met, I didn't think I'd get along with my cousins. And now we were the best of friends. Then I saw Alec and his brother, Antoine. I remembered when they were being so mean, but now they were smiling and really friendly. I guess that meant things were a lot better for them at home.

Besides all of that, I didn't have to worry about keeping things inside me anymore. Brooke and I were able to talk about stuff that might have kept us from being friends. So I learned that I could tell her how I really felt. I always thought that she was pretty. But I just found out that she thought I was pretty too. I was really surprised when Alec said I was pretty and cool too. Hearing that gave me butter-flies in my tummy.

This was just a perfect day. My parents were happy. My friends were here. I had loads of presents that I couldn't wait to open, and I knew God had made me just the way He wanted me to be. When I put everything together—life was oh, so sweet!

Letter to Dad

Dear Dad,

Well, I told you about Sam before. But then we got scared when she had an **emergency**. So Mom and Daddy Derek took her to the hospital. Sam has been under a lot of **pressure** from her friends to lose weight. She got sick because she wasn't eating right. Thankfully, a doctor is taking care of her now, and she's gonna be okay.

Daddy Derek prayed with us kids, and we all feel better. Dad, I've learned that I'm okay just the way that I am because God made me in His image.

My cousins, Drake and Sadie, learned to love themselves too. They are fun to be with, Dad. They taught me some **concepts** from their geography lessons. I learned the **equator** goes around the earth.

Sadie got **sentimental** when she was teaching me, but Drake told her to quit being so mushy and tell me about the **prime meridian**. I learned it goes up and down the earth.

Most of all, I've learned that I have people who love me. That means I can feel **positive** about myself because I want to be open and honest with you, Mom, Daddy Derek, and Jesus.

> Your daughter,
> Miss Growing-Up Morgan

Word Search

```
P  I  L  E  Q  U  A  T  O  R  L  S
R  P  M  L  P  M  O  C  H  A  G  T
E  R  E  I  O  B  L  O  T  B  E  E
S  I  R  T  S  K  A  N  R  E  O  R
S  M  I  J  I  O  E  C  K  A  G  U
I  E  D  B  T  M  P  E  A  U  R  S
N  X  I  Z  I  A  L  P  E  T  A  S
G  O  A  T  V  P  A  T  L  I  P  E
N  W  N  D  E  S  Y  S  U  F  H  R
R  E  M  E  R  G  E  N  C  Y  Y  P
S  G  L  O  B  E  W  O  R  L  D  Q
V  B  T  Y  S  E  Q  U  A  T  E  U
```

CONCEPTS

EMERGENCY

EQUATOR

POSITIVE

PRESSURE

PRIME MERIDIAN (two words)

SENTIMENTAL

Words to Know and Learn

1) e·mer·gen·cy (ĭ-mûr'jən-sē) *noun*
A serious situation or occurrence that happens unexpectedly and demands immediate action

2) pres·sure (prĕsh'ər) *noun*
A strong influence on the mind or emotions

3) con·cepts (kŏn'sĕpt') *noun*
Thoughts or notions

4) e·qua·tor (ĭ-kwā'tər) *noun*
The imaginary great circle around the earth that is halfway between the North and South Poles

5) sen·ti·men·tal (sĕn'tə-mĕn'tl) *adjective*
Feeling emotional about something

6) prime meridian (prīm mə-rĭd'ē-ən) *noun*
The imaginary circle around the Earth that passes through Greenwich, England. It is used to measure longitude east and west.

7) pos·i·tive (pŏz'ĭ-tĭv) *adjective*
Favorable, good, approving

Something Special

Stephanie Perry Moore
Discussion Questions

1. Morgan Love wants to fit in so badly that when her classmates make fun of the kid with special needs, Morgan joins in and truly hurts the boy's feelings. Do you think Morgan was right to make him feel bad just to fit in? How would you feel if you were being picked on?

2. Morgan gets in big trouble at school. Do you think her parents should punish her? When you do something wrong, how do you try and fix it?

3. Morgan's parents argue over how to discipline her. Do you think Morgan is right to want to make things better between them? How can you help keep peace in your home?

4. Morgan and her cousins all have something they don't like about themselves. Do you think the make-believe land they create helps them? What do you ever imagine or dream?

5. When Morgan walks in on her cousin Sam making herself sick, Sam asks Morgan to keep her secret. Do you think it was right for Morgan not to tell her mother what she knows? What would you do if someone told you to keep a secret that could bring harm?

6. At church, Morgan learns about self-esteem. What do you think she learns? How do you feel about yourself?

7. Morgan wishes she looked like her best buddy, Brooke. Do you think she was right to open up and tell her friend about the way she felt? How can you have a better friendship with your good friend?

Word Search Solutions

Chapter 1 Solution

```
R  E  A  D  U  N  G  G  O  O  D  B
O  O  K  S  T  H  A  T  S  B  S  T
R  J  Y  F  I  L  A  U  Q  S  I  D
E  P  A  R  T  I  C  I  P  A  T  E
S  E  H  M  Q  U  H  C  P  E  P  N
O  R  E  O  U  C  A  R  A  Z  A  I
L  R  A  R  I  X  R  E  P  I  T  M
U  Y  L  G  L  D  A  U  A  R  C  R
T  S  T  A  T  E  C  L  E  P  I  E
I  J  H  N  S  M  T  B  J  L  C  T
O  A  Y  D  I  G  E  S  T  Z  I  E
N  M  O  M  O  O  R  E  L  E  A  D
```

CHARACTER

CRUEL

DETERMINED

DIGEST

DISQUALIFY

HEALTHY

PARTICIPATE

Chapter 2 Solution

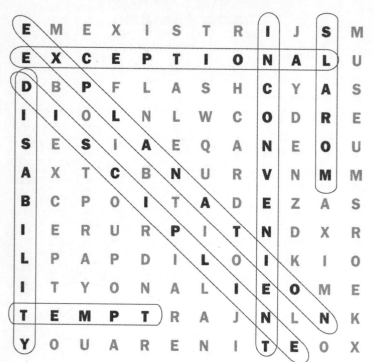

DISABILITY

DISCIPLINE

EXCEPTIONAL

EXPLANATION

INCONVENIENT

MORALS

TEMPT

Chapter 3 Solution

CENTERPIECE

DISAPPOINT

HESITATE

MOTION

PLEASANT

PREDICT

ORDEAL

Chapter 4 Solution

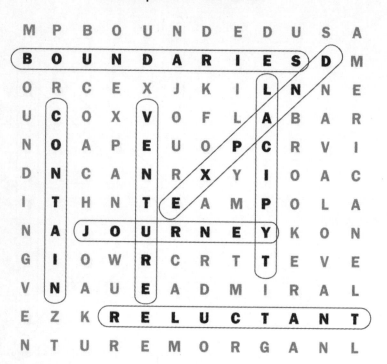

CONTAIN

BOUNDARIES

EXPAND

JOURNEY

RELUCTANT

TYPICAL

VENTURE

Chapter 5 Solution

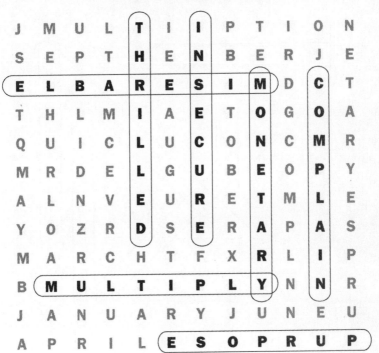

COMPLAIN

INSECURE

MISERABLE

MONETARY

MULTIPLY

PURPOSE

THRILLED

Chapter 6 Solution

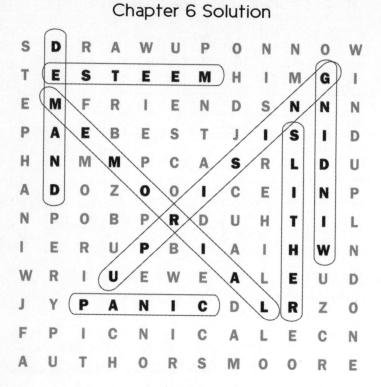

DEMAND

ESTEEM

MEMORIAL

PANIC

SLITHER

UPRISING

WINDING

Chapter 7 Solution

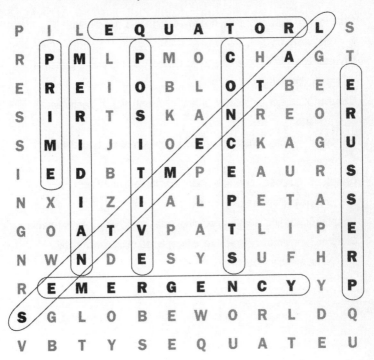

CONCEPTS

EMERGENCY

EQUATOR

POSITIVE

PRESSURE

PRIME MERIDIAN (two words)

SENTIMENTAL

Word Keep Book

Chapter 1: digest, character, healthy, determined, participate, disqualify, cruel

Chapter 2: explanation, exceptional, disability, inconvenience, morals, discipline, tempt

Chapter 3: predict, disappoint, ordeal, pleasant, motion, centerpiece, hesitate

Chapter 4: typical, reluctant, expand, journey, venture, boundaries, contain

Chapter 5: purpose, miserable, monetary, thrilled, multiply, complain, insecure

Chapter 6: uprising, demand, winding, esteem, slither, memorial, panic

Chapter 7: emergency, pressure, concepts, equator, sentimental, prime meridian, positive

Worksheets

4 Bonus Pages

(1 English, 1 Math, 1 Science, 1 Social Studies)

Worksheet 1

English: Adjectives

Adjectives: Adjectives are words that describe a noun.

Example: The smart girl got an A on her test.

The word *smart* is an adjective. It describes the noun *girl*.

Directions: In each sentence, circle the adjective that describes the underlined noun.

1) Trey and Billy played with the round ball.
2) Mrs. Hardy placed the white chalk on the board.
3) Brooke's birthday is on the fourth day of June.
4) Daddy Derek's car has a flat tire.
5) Morgan held the book in her right arm.
6) Alec wore a blue shirt.
7) The green snow cone was Tim's favorite.
8) Mama cooked buttermilk pancakes and bacon.
9) My dad is sailing on the Navy ship.
10) Papa loves to drive his red convertible.

Worksheet 2
Math: Multiplication

0s–3s Speed Multiplication

Any number times 0 always equals 0.

Example:

$5 \times 0 = 0$

Any number times 1 equals that same number.

$3 \times 1 = 3$

Any number times 2 equals that number doubled.

$5 \times 2 = 10 \ (5 + 5 = 10)$

Any number times 3 equals that number tripled.

$4 \times 3 = 12 \ (4 + 4 + 4 = 12)$

Directions: After you have studied the multiplication facts for 0, 1, 2, and 3, see how quickly you can answer these problems.

1) $3 \times 9 =$ 2) $2 \times 8 =$ 3) $2 \times 2 =$ 4) $2 \times 5 =$

5) $3 \times 10 =$ 6) $3 \times 7 =$ 7) $2 \times 12 =$ 8) $3 \times 12 =$

9) $2 \times 3 =$ 10) $3 \times 3 =$ 11) $2 \times 10 =$ 12) $2 \times 11 =$

13) $0 \times 4 =$ 14) $3 \times 1 =$ 15) $3 \times 6 =$ 16) $1 \times 1 =$

17) $1 \times 11 =$ 18) $3 \times 11 =$ 19) $5 \times 2 =$ 20) $2 \times 0 =$

Worksheet 3
Science: Planets

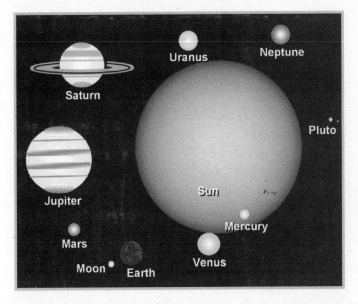

Directions: Study the planets and find which planet best fits each question.

1) This planet is seventh from the sun. _____
2) This planet has rings around it. _____
3) This planet is closest to the sun. _____
4) This planet is the smallest one. _____
5) This planet is the one we live on. _____
6) This planet is the largest. _____
7) This planet gets very hot. _____
8) This planet has a red and stony desert._____
9) This planet has 13 known moons. _____
10) All the planets revolve around this object. _____

(picture from http://www.solarsystempictures.net/)

Worksheet 4
Social Studies: Continents and Oceans

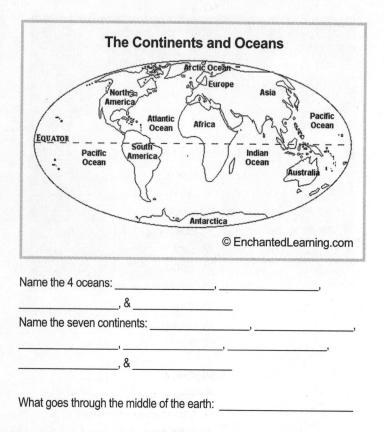

The Continents and Oceans

Arctic Ocean

Europe

North America

Asia

Pacific Ocean

Atlantic Ocean

Africa

EQUATOR

Pacific Ocean

South America

Indian Ocean

Australia

Antarctica

© EnchantedLearning.com

Name the 4 oceans: _____, _____,

_____, & _____

Name the seven continents: _____, _____,

_____, _____, _____,

_____, & _____

What goes through the middle of the earth: _____

Source:
http://www.proteacher.com/cgi-bin/outsidesite.cgi?id=15215&external=
http://www.enChantédlearning.com/geography/continents/quiz.shtml&origin

Answer Keys

Worksheet 1

1) round
2) white
3) fourth
4) flat
5) right
6) blue
7) green
8) buttermilk
9) Navy
10) red

Worksheet 2

1) 27
2) 16
3) 4
4) 10
5) 30
6) 21
7) 24
8) 36
9) 6
10) 9
11) 20
12) 22
13) 0

14) 3
15) 18
16) 1
17) 11
18) 33
19) 10
20) 0

Worksheet 3

1) Uranus
2) Saturn
3) Mercury
4) Pluto
5) Earth
6) Jupiter
7) Venus
8) Mars
9) Neptune
10) Sun

Worksheet 4

1) Arctic Ocean	2) Pacific Ocean
3) Indian Ocean	4) Atlantic Ocean
5) North America	6) South America
7) Africa	8) Asia
9) Australia	10) Europe
11) Antarctica	12) Equator

Credit to: http://www.homeschoolmath.net/worksheets/grade_2.php

Acknowledgments

I looked in the mirror today and didn't like what I saw. I know I'm getting older, but who wants a few grey hairs, a larger tummy, and a sagging chin? No one. But after spending Teen Read Week with several great schools in the Atlantic Public School System, I learned that I had to practice what I preached.

I told many young people to look at life from the positive point of view. I told them to learn to manage their issues. I told them they are special; that they just have to let their weaknesses become their strengths.

Well, since I told others that, then I had to get over myself. So I now look at my grey hair as my wisdom growing. My larger tummy means the Lord has allowed me to not miss a meal. I'm not disappointed with my sagging chin because it's a family trait, and I love my family.

Bottom line, God created us all, and He doesn't make junk. My point is this: the Lord created you in His image, and He is perfect. Concentrate on that, and you'll be more than fine.

Here is a special thank you to all the people who help me concentrate and create purposeful stories.

To my parents, Dr. Franklin and Shirley Perry, I feel special that God chose for me such loving parents.

To my Moody Team/Lift Every Voice family, especially Greg Thornton, I feel special that years ago you saw promise in my work and gave me a chance.

To my precious cousin and assistant, Ciara Roundtree, I feel special that though you are in college with much to do, you still make the time to help me.

To my friends who gave input into this series: Vannessa Davis Griggs, Marjorie Kimbrough, Dr. Thelma Day, Dr. Deborah C. Thomas, Michele Clark Jenkins, Denise Hendricks, Sherri McGee McCovey, Lois Barney, Veronica Evans, Sophia Nelson, Laurie Weaver, Dr. Taiwanna Brown-Bolds, Lakeba Williams, Jackie Dixon, Jenell Clark, Sarah Lundy, Vickie Randall, Christine Nixon, and Deborah Bradley, I feel special that you care enough for me to always be there when I need a friend.

To my children, Dustyn, Sydni, and Sheldyn, I feel special that I'm your mom.

To my hubby, Derrick C. Moore, I feel special that you chose me to be your mate for life.

To my new young readers, I feel special that—of all the

books you could be reading—you're reading mine.

And, to my heavenly Father, I feel special that You have allowed me to write for You, and I pray every reader learns the purpose You have for them and learns how to live it.

THE DOUBLE DUTCH CLUB

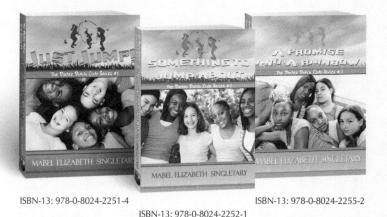

ISBN-13: 978-0-8024-2251-4

ISBN-13: 978-0-8024-2252-1

ISBN-13: 978-0-8024-2255-2

Six friends from Grover Cleveland Elementary School have one thing in common: they love Double Dutch. As the Double Dutch Club finds out, the road to the competition isn't easy, but it is definitely worth the ride. When it comes to friendship (and to Double Dutch) they've learned what to do—just jump in!

Lift Every Voice Books

Lift every voice and sing
Till earth and heaven ring,
Ring with the harmonies of Liberty;
Let our rejoicing rise
High as the listening skies,
Let it resound loud as the rolling sea.
Sing a song full of the faith that the dark past has taught us,
Sing a song full of the hope that the present has brought us,
Facing the rising sun of our new day begun
Let us march on till victory is won.

The Black National Anthem, written by James Weldon Johnson in 1900, captures the essence of Lift Every Voice Books. Lift Every Voice Books is an imprint of Moody Publishers that celebrates a rich culture and great heritage of faith, based on the foundation of eternal truth—God's Word. We endeavor to restore the fabric of the African-American soul and reclaim the indomitable spirit that kept our forefathers true to God in spite of insurmountable odds.

We are Lift Every Voice Books—Christ-centered books and resources for restoring the African-American soul.

For more information on other books and products
written and produced from a biblical perspective, go to
www.lifteveryvoicebooks.com or write to:

Lift Every Voice Books
820 N. LaSalle Boulevard
Chicago, IL 60610
www.lifteveryvoicebooks.com